Moonglade
and
Other Stories

I0525487

by

Frank Castelluccio

SYNTHETIC
PROPHETIC

"*It's Only Sex, After All*" was first published in *Pangyrus*. "Hollywood Endings" was first published in *RFD Magazine* and *Made in L.A. Vol. 5: Vantage Points*. "Martha's House" was first published in *Avalon Literary Review*.`

Library of Congress Control Number: 2024919626

SYNTHETIC PROPHETIC ⇌
Kingston, New York, USA
www.syntheticprophetic.com

ISBN: 979-8-9856091-5-8

Printed in the United States.

Contents

For my mother, Anna.
Sei sempre nel mio cuore.

Hollywood Endings

The first night they met, Ikal walked Roy home and they kissed in the courtyard enveloped by the scent of night-blooming jasmine, while the captivatingly warm Santa Ana winds danced furiously around them, sealing that first kiss with a magic neither had ever known. It was in the Hollywood Hills, in a bright pink 1940s apartment building reminiscent of a Mexican hacienda, that the two lovers first found happiness. The courtyard was an oasis filled with luscious palm trees, regal aloe plants, tall polished jades, glamorous ferns, and a majestic purple bougainvillea that had, long before Roy and Ikal were ever there, blanketed the walls of the two-story buildings to form what looked like a horseshoe. Along the borders, in the shaded areas, multicolored impatiens stood at attention waiting for their daily watering. Dozens of terra cotta pots left by prior residents brimmed with cactus plants and unfulfilled dreams. This was the place where their love story began.

Ikal's journey to that moment started on a cool, dry morning at dawn in Santiago El Pinar. In his room, his record player spun as the needle skipped in a lazy rhythm on the final groove of the record that Ikal had listened to over and over the night before. "Yo No Naci Para Amar" was a tune about a young man who believed he was never meant to love anyone. He turned the player off, put the disc back in the sleeve, and stacked his records atop the cabinet, making sure they were completely aligned. His textbooks on drafting and architecture sat neatly on his desk, and his hand trembled as it passed over the covers in a goodbye caress. He clicked off the reading light, shouldered the bulging backpack, and took one last look out the window. Santiago El Pinar, a small town in the Chiapas region of Mexico, was his birthplace a ghost town filled with living souls trying to escape.

His mother stood before the stove, a wooden spoon in hand. As he walked into the kitchen, the familiar morning scents greeted him: freshly ground coffee brewing, sweet anise rolls baking, and eggs sizzling in the large frying pan that never seemed to leave its place on the stove.

"Mijo, estas seguro? Tal vez tu padre pueda ayudarte," his mother said, wanting to know if he was sure, maybe his father could help. She tried to avoid his eyes as she wiped the kitchen table.

"Me tengo que ir," responded Ikal. "No puedo ser un narco. Me mataran si no hago lo que dicen." If he stayed, he'd be forced to work for the drug cartel. He had to leave to protect his family.

She finally looked him in the eyes. "No se por que pregunte. Se que estas haciendo lo correcto." She knew he was doing the right thing even before she had asked the question.

2

She walked him to the door, took his arms, and turned him toward her. Looking deeply into his eyes, she made the sign of the cross on his chest to bless him and said, "Que Dios te cuide." Without another word, she opened the door, releasing him into the unknown of the deserts and the mountains that, until now, had always inscribed a limit for their family.

It took weeks to make the journey. With every step he took, the unforgiving sun kept reminding Ikal that death could come at any moment, without mercy or reason.

He would never speak to anyone about the things he had done to gain favor to make the crossing, or the things that had been done to others, or of those that perished. Days of walking, waiting; always hungry, always thirsty, and so tired … all snipped from the reel of memory, dropped to the cutting room floor.

The first thing he did when he arrived in the City of Angels was phone his family, to get word to them that all was fine. He was well, and he had arrived safely.

East L.A. was not what he expected. His cousin's building looked like a prison with all its windows dressed in security bars. He heard children shrieking through the walls and wondered if they ever played outside. The two-bedroom apartment was already crowded with his cousin's children and other members of his wife's family who had recently made the trip from Mexico. Ikal would have to sleep on the floor in the hallway on a twin mattress purchased from a secondhand shop.

On the day he arrived, he stood naked in the bathroom looking in the mirror affixed to the back of the door. He tentatively touched his left upper thigh and turned to look at the side of his body, which was tender and bruised from bouncing around inside the trunk on the way from San Diego with three other men. He sat on the edge of the bath and looked at the blisters on the bottom of his feet, strands of bloodied sock still stuck to his flesh. He lifted his hands to his face and looked at them closely. They were scratched and blistered from never releasing his grip on the backpack he had carried. He had done his best to clean up during the journey but, based on his cousin's wife's reaction, he knew how he must have smelled.

"Mijo! Por favor! Ahi esta el baño, ve!" she had said, pointing to the bathroom.

He stood for a long time in the shower, watching the water turn brown as it poured down his body, spin around the rim of the drain, and then disappear. He looked at his hands again, placed both over his mouth, and let out a muffled scream.

Meanwhile, three thousand miles away, on the other side of the country, Roy was anxiously getting ready for his trip to Los Angeles. He forced the zippers closed on his two suitcases. He had packed, unpacked, and repacked at least a dozen times, unsure whether he was taking too much or too little. He looked at the patchwork of photos and posters of his favorite actors and movies plastered on all four walls of his bedroom and smiled. He had always been certain that in a past life he had lived in Los Angeles and been part of the Hollywood Dream Factory. He knew he wanted to be an actor and was assured of his readiness after years at the Actors Studio taking classes in voice, movement, and character development, searching for his inner truth, and honing his craft in community theater. It was time to make it in Hollywood!

Roy had been planning this trip all his life but always postponed it one more year on his mother's request not to leave her. Having just turned thirty, he couldn't wait any longer. He finally convinced his mother that it would only be for six months, and that he'd return. Initially she accepted that condition. "Okay, if you promise you will be back. Don't make me come and get you!" she'd warned.

"I promise, Ma, I will come back," he said as his mother stroked his hair away from his forehead and smiled.

"You've always reminded me of a young Tyrone Power with your hair slicked back."

Roy's sister may have been more supportive of his decision had it not left her alone to care for their mother. "But you will be back, right?" his sister asked in a panic.

"I have to go now, or I never will. I know that." He offered a half-hearted smile to reassure her, but he could see that she knew he would not return.

His mother stood at the front door, arms splayed, a human barrier. She begged and pleaded for him not to go. "I'll lose you forever! I won't be able to go on for another day!"

"Ma! Really? C'mon, you know you are everything to me, but I have to do this."

She moved away from the door crying, giving him just enough space to pass. He kissed her on the forehead and promised once again he'd be back.

His heart wrenched when he started the car and pulled out of the driveway, but at last he was driving down the street. He looked in the rearview mirror and saw his mother in the middle of the road bent over in tears. He slowed for a moment, placing his hand on the gear shift, but instead of turning back, he reached for the mirror, looked at his reflection, combed his hair back, and tilted the mirror down so he could no longer see her as he drove away.

He would later tell Ikal that his drive was like floating on a magic carpet. He barely rested, and his excitement grew with each state line he crossed. When he entered California from Nevada, he burst into song, belting out "California Here I Come." He sang it repeatedly until his voice sounded like mice squeaking. From US Highway 101, he took exit 9A — Cahuenga Blvd. — Hollywood Bowl. He stopped at the first telephone booth he could find and called his mother.

"Ma! I'm here! It's exactly what I have been imagining all these years. One day we will make the trip together. It's gonna be great! You'll see!" he said excitedly.

"That's nice. I'm happy for you, really," she said flatly. "I need my heart meds renewed. Can you call your sister and tell her? She doesn't know her ass from her elbow when it comes to taking care of me." And then she hung up.

※

On that first night, Ikal and Roy shared all that is kept in the depths of one's soul, all the secrets that are never voiced to anyone else for fear of being judged. They seemed to grasp all that had appeared to them between wake and sleep, all that had waited, hidden just beyond the shroud.

The garden became their temple, and they both cherished it for what they experienced and what they shared. In that courtyard, they found their home. Together they'd take care of it.

At first, they met every three or four days, and then every other day. Ikal would show up showered, his shirt ironed and smelling like patchouli, always sighing once the door was opened — as if reading his first line of a scene.

"I'm glad you are here. I didn't know if it was good for me to come over," Ikal said as he rubbed Roy's earlobe with his thumb and index finger.

"You say that every time. You know I'm waiting for you!" Roy said as he took Ikal's hand and kissed the palm of it.

Ikal sometimes stayed the night, but he always left before the sun came up.

Roy didn't know exactly where Ikal lived. He'd told him it was somewhere down La Brea Avenue but never gave him the address. "I'm beginning to think you have another man hidden somewhere. That's why you never give me your address. Are you cheating on me?" Roy asked, half kidding, half serious.

"I would never cheat on you!" Ikal said, his brow creased

with consternation. "Ever! If either of us ever falls in love with someone else, it must be said. No cheating, ever!"

Roy looked at him, smiled, and caressed his face.

Their usual place, Hoy's Wok, was at Hollywood Boulevard and Cahuenga. It had four tables inside and two on the sidewalk. Roy called it a restaurant, but it was really a take-out joint. The windows needed to be cleaned, and the tables screamed out for tablecloths and flowers, but the place was sweet. For five dollars they'd get pork fried rice or lo mein, chicken with garlic sauce, or boneless spareribs, tiny things that Roy referred to as "pork chips." He would stare in amazement at the amount of hot sauce Ikal put on everything. "Doesn't that bother your stomach? Do you even taste the food?" Roy would always ask.

"Yes, I can taste it. I'm used to eating spicy. This is really not that hot," Ikal would respond, without looking up, as beads of sweat glittered on his face and forehead.

If they could scrape together forty dollars between them, they would head to Mickey's in West Hollywood, the bar where they had met. When the pair walked in, both men and women turned to look. Roy was fair-skinned, tall, and lean, with jet-black hair and deep green eyes. Roy's confident and elegant gait often made those who walked past him wonder whether they had just seen their favorite movie actor. Ikal was also tall, but his skin was silky caramel, and he took pride in his muscular frame, earned by the hard manual jobs he accepted (but needed to constantly change due to his undocumented status). When it was his turn to be carded at the door,

Ikal nervously handed his fake I.D. to the bouncers, but they barely looked at it. "Welcome," they'd whisper while handing it back to him, gazing with bedroom eyes. "Go ahead — maybe a drink later?" His piercing black eyes and long black hair captivated everyone. The bartenders nicknamed him "Mayan Prince."

Getting there before 7:00 p.m. meant tap beer for a dollar, served in plastic cups. They drank several, and when late afternoon turned to evening, they would order Long Island Iced Tea. The combination of vodka, tequila, rum, and gin always did the trick. By this time, Roy headed for the dance floor, but it took Ikal at least another drink before he could get up the nerve to dance. He would stand on the side and smile as Roy jumped up and down, spinning and yelling, "I LOVE THIS SONG!" Roy would then drag Ikal onto the dance floor, where the two danced until their bodies were soaked with sweat. When Tammy Wynette and The KLF sang "Justified & Ancient," it signaled that the night was over and the bar was closing.

Once outside, their ears buzzed and the sounds of faraway muffled voices surrounded them as men and women left the club. Ikal would then take Roy's hand and insist they go to the beach. Roy would cite the late hour but relent when Ikal pleaded that they go look at the stars. Roy would smile and say, "Only because it's like a movie."

The next day, hungover and exhausted, they would always make the same agreement. "We cannot go out when we have to work the next day," Roy would scold. "From now on, we go out only on the weekends." Somehow, they were always able to find those forty dollars, and the following week it would inevitably happen again.

On those rare days when they had a day off together, Roy planned trips to his favorite Hollywood sites: cemeteries. There they would stroll past the graves of long-gone actors, Roy tutoring Ikal on their place in film history. "You see, the thirties and forties were the golden age of Hollywood. That's when stars were really stars. When they made the classics! It was glamorous. It's exciting! You can feel it, right? The magic?" Roy would say.

"Exciting? Doesn't that mean happy? Everyone is dead here. I don't know why we should be happy," Ikal responded.

"You don't get it. It's not about happiness. It's different for me. I grew up watching these people. It's like I know them personally." Roy would take Ikal by the hand and pull him about the cemetery. Then he would add how each legend had died. "Fatty Arbuckle, sad story, dead at forty-six of a heart attack — he never really made a comeback after being accused of rape. John Barrymore, he's over there, died of cirrhosis of the liver — great actor. Oh! And over there, that's Peg Entwistle … poor thing jumped off the Hollywood sign … only twenty-four, couldn't make it once talkies came in. But she's a star now! Yup, those were the years when Hollywood was really Hollywood!"

Ikal smiled at Roy's excitement. "I don't really understand. It's all so sad, but if it makes you happy, then I'm happy for you."

Roy and Ikal celebrated their first Thanksgiving together. Roy's mother was not happy; it was their first time apart on a holiday. Ikal and Roy ate dry turkey sandwiches with lots of mayonnaise, drank ice-cold beer, ate pumpkin pie bought at the supermarket, and made love throughout the day. "I am very thankful that you're here with me," Roy whispered in Ikal's ear. "This is the first Thanksgiving that I'm not depressed."

"Maybe next year you can make a real dinner? I see on the commercials they have a lot more food on the table," Ikal teased while chewing on the last of his sandwich.

"Shut up! This is all we can do this year. It will be better next year, you'll see. I have a bunch of catering gigs lined up. We'll make this Christmas special."

Early December, on a ninety-degree day in Bel Air, Roy drove up a long curving driveway to a massive mansion sheathed with thousands of miniature white lights made redundant by the piercing sun. Fake snow had been strategically placed on the perfectly manicured grass, sprinkled around bushes, and piled on flowering plants so as to cover the blooms. Inside, the house was a Christmas wonderland; the air was scented with pine, and Bing Crosby crooned "White Christmas." On duty, Roy stood by a blazing fireplace in the middle of the living room holding a tray of hors d'oeuvres. Like the rest of the staff, he wore a red silk bow tie and a red velvet tuxedo jacket. Although the air conditioning blasted throughout the house, Roy sweated profusely. He caught a glimpse of two women in fur coats standing by the sixteen-foot Christmas tree as a photographer snapped their picture. Other guests, wearing wool sweaters, hats, and scarves, waited alongside for their photos to be taken. To no one in particular Roy suddenly blurted, "You people are nuts, batshit crazy! I'm going home for Christmas!"

He called his sister and asked if she would help with the airfare. "I'll pay you back in a couple of months. I promise."

"Like you were coming back in six months, right? Fine. It'll be a break from Mom," she replied.

He broke the news to Ikal delicately. "I'll be back in a week. I just have to go and see my mom for a few days, and then I will come back for New Year. We'll dance all night long!"

"Your family is important to you. It's good that you can go. I would too if I could." Ikal held his breath and pretended to wipe dust from his eyes.

The night before Roy left, they went out for drinks. Ikal hadn't eaten much that day and gulped three Long Island Iced Teas in quick succession. Nothing Roy did could get Ikal on the dance floor. Stone-faced, he sat watching Roy, until he rose and walked out of the bar, unnoticed.

Roy spotted his broad shoulders in the small park across the street, where Ikal sat alone on a bench.

"Please come back," Ikal said without looking at Roy. And then a sob erupted from his lungs, and he bawled so hard he couldn't catch his breath.

Roy sat and held him. "I could never leave you; of course I'm coming back. Where is this coming from?"

"I have no one that cares for me. Only you! Only you! You

can't leave me! I can't go home anymore. You are my home." Ikal was slurring and clutching Roy like someone about to fall off a cliff.

"I'll always come home to you, always," Roy said as he wrapped his arms around Ikal. He rocked him back and forth until Ikal finally stopped crying. That was the last time Roy ever saw Ikal cry.

The next day they drove to LAX. Neither mentioned the night before. As Roy's flight was called, he stood before the gate, looked at Ikal, and said, "I've been waiting all my life for you. Nothing is going to keep me from coming back."

Six days later, Roy walked up the ramp to the same spot and found Ikal in an ironed shirt, smelling of patchouli, and holding a bouquet of flowers from Ralph's grocery store.

"You're a nut!" Roy said as he hugged him.

Ikal rubbed Roy's earlobe until they were in the car and then they kissed. "It's good you are back."

"It's good to be back. I couldn't wait to come home. It's time to take the next step."

Roy spent days getting the apartment in shape so that Ikal would feel at home. He cleaned, made space in the closet, bought new towels and sheets, and even regrouted the bathtub. It was the first time in Roy's life that he would live with someone other than his family.

A car pulled up at the corner of Hillside and El Cerrito

Place. A young man dressed in black jeans and a black shirt dropped boxes on the sidewalk, and joggers on their way to Runyon Canyon zigzagged around them. Roy still had no idea where Ikal had been living, or with whom. He wanted to make the stranger feel welcome, so he said, "Hi! I'm Roy!"

The man got back in the car, waved to Ikal, and said, "Orale wey." Then drove away.

"Who was that?" Roy asked. "Why didn't you introduce me? Why didn't he say hello?"

"Just a guy. He had to leave. It's not important," Ikal said as he started hauling things in.

"It's important to me. In my world, people introduce people to each other. Everything with you is so cloak-and-dagger. I feel like I don't exist sometimes, like you don't tell anyone who I am or what I mean to you."

"Why do we have to tell anyone? As long as we know who we are to each other and what we mean to one another, that's all that is important. It's no one's business."

Roy stood for a moment. He lifted a box, shook his head, and followed Ikal.

Their life became an unorganized routine. They worked when work was available. They went out to clubs and window-shopped at trendy boutiques on Melrose Avenue, never able to afford anything. They ate dollar Chinese food and celebrated birthdays with inexpensive gifts, always promising that next year would be better. One late afternoon while sitting on the beach waiting for the blue sky to turn dark, Roy announced, "I'm going to stop thinking of this crazy idea of becoming an actor." He paused, waiting for Ikal to disagree with him, but when he said nothing, Roy continued. "I've fallen out of love with acting. I'm not even sure why I wanted to be an actor. I like the attention, but … perhaps if I had come here in my twenties." He looked at Ikal, expecting something.

"What do you want to do?" asked Ikal.

"I want to make money. I'm tired of just scraping by. I want to buy those things we see. I want to eat at a real restaurant. I want to be able to pay the electric bill!" They both laughed. Roy continued, "Maybe we can open a business together, right?"

"That would be nice," Ikal mumbled. "It's going to be hard with no money."

"That's what credit cards are for. And maybe you can start taking classes at night, study architecture," Roy mused. "You always say you want to be an architect."

"When I was a small boy, I always drew houses. I see how they look inside of them in my head. It would be like my dream come true if I could do that," Ikal responded in a lively, bright tone.

"We just have to figure out what we can do that's going to be successful," Roy said. "We'll make it work; you'll see. We've come this far together — we'll make it together. And once you get your green card, we're going to travel the world. It's going to be amazing! You'll see."

Neither looked into the other's eyes as Roy spoke those

words. Instead, they looked at the ocean while Roy made small circles in the sand with his finger. Ikal reached out and took Roy's hand in his.

"Maybe," Ikal said softly.

Unhappiness took hold of them at some point, but neither could recall when. Roy hadn't been able to find a new career that inspired him. He still scraped by with catering jobs, organizing homes of the wealthy, and living the life of an unemployed actor who no longer had the dream of becoming a star. Ikal's frustrations grew with each job he had to leave whenever someone in human resources found out his documents were fake. Defeated, he would need to search for another unfulfilling job yet again. Their desperation boiled over, searching for someone to blame, and naturally they went after each other.

Both played a good game of chess. They instinctively understood which piece would be moved and precisely when it would take place, so neither could ever call checkmate.

"Have you decided about leaving?" Roy managed to say, attempting to hide his anger but failing miserably. He stood by the kitchen sink, having removed the Teflon from the frying pan he'd been scrubbing for an hour.

Ikal had spent the night out — again. Not with anyone special, Roy was sure of that. Still, it drove him mad not knowing and not having been warned in advance. He'd had another sleepless night wondering whether Ikal was safe.

"No, not yet," Ikal responded quietly. "I don't know if I

should leave. Do you want me to go?"

Neither was ready to commit to leaving or to staying. Roy had always thought if Ikal could, somehow, become a legal resident that maybe, just maybe, his demons could be exorcised, and he wouldn't live in constant fear.

"Don't start that crap with me!" Roy exploded, slamming the now decimated frying pan against the sink. Roy found Ikal's indecision exasperating. They were stuck on a merry-go-round trying to jump off, but both too hesitant of taking that first step, afraid of falling.

"And now you start!" Ikal replied, crossing his arms.

"I won't make any more of your decisions! I've had it! You hear me?" Roy yelled. "This time I've had it!"

Roy manipulated Ikal's feelings by detailing all that he'd done for him, all he'd given him so he would stay. "I went into bankruptcy to pay for your attorneys. They all promised they would find a way to get you a green card. And when that didn't pan out, I borrowed money from my family to pay a woman to marry you. It wasn't my fault she changed her mind. And now you are ready to abandon me because you can't put up with me, because you find me difficult?"

"I'll never be what you want," Ikal said. "I never asked you to do anything for me."

"Sure, you never did. But you wanted a green card, you wanted to be legal. And I did it for you, and now this is how you repay me. Ready to walk out just when I need your help the most?"

"But do you take care of me because you love me," Ikal

asked resentfully, "or because you pity me?"

It continued this way until the room got quiet. Roy walked outside and sat on the steps leading down to the garden. There he smoked a cigarette and cried silently, wiping away one tear after the next, annoyed at their wetness.

Then Ikal stepped outside and sat beside him. "We need to water the impatiens. It was very hot today." Ikal put his arm around Roy and rubbed his ear.

"Yeah, I know. They look like they are about to drop dead." Roy leaned his head on Ikal's chest. "It's getting more and more difficult taking care of everything ..."

In solitude, Roy brooded on their five years together. It seemed like a lifetime. Five years of arguing, of loving, of making plans that never came to be, of making love, of throwing empty (and sometimes full) bottles of beer against walls. Five years of hoping that the other would change, of wishing that discussions of money, or lack thereof, were not always excuses to rip each other apart. He wished that the differences in their cultures were not justifications of their incompatibility. Whenever Ikal played Banda or Ranchera music, Roy would inevitably lower the sound saying that the "yelling" gave him a headache. And when Roy would make Ikal sit through one of the many romantic movies he watched, Ikal would comment on the unrealistic premises and eventually fall asleep. They simply never saw eye to eye.

But sometimes, when they fell into their four-poster bed and Ikal put his head near Roy's and rubbed his earlobe with his thumb and forefinger, they were both brought back to that place where they were alone, completely apart from the world, completely devoid of any problem or difference. How they clung to each other. Was it out of love or was it out of fear of being alone? Neither could make sense of it.

The magic of that first kiss on that first night so many nights ago became a legend. That moment could no longer sustain their existence together. Both were tired of hearing the other's explanations, excuses, or resolutions.

As a couple, they emitted mixed social messages. Gregarious Roy had always welcomed strangers with open arms, but Ikal was cautious of people and kept mostly to himself. Ikal believed Roy was too quick to trust — that was how you ended up getting hurt. Roy blamed Ikal's standoffishness and mistrust of people as the reason they had no friends.

The only exception was Greg and Bert, an older couple who lived across the courtyard. Greg and Bert had been in Hollywood for many years, having run away from their strict Baptist families in Baton Rouge.

Greg and Roy often confided in and trusted each other, while Bert and Ikal, though cordial and friendly, kept their cards close to their chests, reserved and skeptical. According to Greg, he and Bert never argued, they discussed. "It's the Southern way," Greg proclaimed in his rich baritone drawl. "It's the only way." But when Greg got really angry at Bert, he'd declare, much in the same fashion as his favorite movie character, Scarlett O'Hara, that Bert was "as useless as a fly on an old man's dick!"

Greg's devotion to help the young couple get through their rough patches seemed sincere, but one day Ikal overheard Greg tell Bert that the only reason he and Roy were together was because they looked "marvelous together, just marvelous!" Then the mean-spirited Greg added, "It's dreadfully sad they haven't a thing in common!"

Roy's stubbornness and histrionics made him unable to simply let go, while Ikal's marbleized emotions and predetermined devotion made him incapable of understanding the concept of breaking up.

"Why can't life be like a Hollywood ending?" Roy once asked Greg.

"Because Hollywood endings are only the beginning, my dear."

The couples often dined together. Roy liked setting a folding table and plastic chairs in the middle of the courtyard. He and Greg strung lights, draped the table with a silver foil tablecloth left over from one of Roy's catering jobs, and scattered petals from the flowers in the garden. Above them, to the right of the Hollywood sign, Yamashiro's restaurant stood on a hill, all lit up. As evening grew dark and the warm wind encircled them, Roy's perfect Hollywood magic moment was set. But as the night progressed, with too many cocktails and bottles of wine, conversations intensified and voices got louder. One misunderstood comment between Ikal and Roy resulted in a screaming match.

"Darlings! Dining with you is like stepping into one of those loathsome scenes between George and Martha in Who's Afraid of Virginia Woolf?" Greg stated grandly.

Bert looked over to Greg disapprovingly and said, "Now, Greg, let the boys be," as he sipped on his double bourbon mint julep.

Roy didn't appreciate the reference but understood it for what it was. Ikal didn't, and that made him more frustrated, insecure, and angry — emotions he took out on Roy.

One night, Greg and Bert returned from dinner, and as they walked through the courtyard, they heard Roy screaming.

"Dear God," Greg mumbled, "those boys are going to kill each other!"

"Let them be!" Bert said. "Live and let live, they'll figure it out." But instead of following Bert inside, Greg stood in the shadows and listened.

"How could you send them our rent money?" Roy yelled.

"I didn't send it all. I'm sorry — they really needed it," Ikal said.

Roy continued yelling, "Why do you always do these things without consulting me first? Why is it always behind my back?"

"I thought I could work extra shifts and have the money back."

"I can't take this anymore! All they do is take, take, take! Never once have they returned any of the money you lent them! Why doesn't your family cross over like everyone else and get jobs?" Roy suddenly stopped and looked at Ikal standing with his hands balled up in fists. Roy had never seen him so angry. They had a rule: Never to go after each other's families. Roy had broken that rule.

Roy took a step back as Ikal advanced on him. But instead of striking Roy, Ikal kicked one of the cats across the room. The cat jumped up looking astonished and crawled under the sofa. Then Ikal walked out.

Furious, Roy ran around the apartment opening cabinets, looking in closets and then under the kitchen sink. Behind the garbage pail, he found the toolbox. He opened it and reached for the hammer. He ran toward the front door but came to an abrupt stop, grabbing his chest. Roy fell to the floor, tried to catch his breath, and then curled into the fetal position.

Ikal didn't see Greg as he ran by him crying. Greg waited for Ikal to leave the courtyard before going into the apartment. When he saw Roy, he yelled, "Jesus! Are you all right? Ya'll are going to be the death of me!"

"I'm okay, I just need a moment." Slowly Roy stood up, looked around the room, and walked to the liquor cabinet. He grabbed a bottle of scotch and poured himself a shot as he had seen leading men in movies so often do moments before their inevitable doom.

"You cannot go on like this. It's madness, do you hear? Madness! No love is worth this much pain." Greg took Roy's hand in his. "You've got to end it. I know the thought is devastating, but you've got to end it!" He paused. "Do you want me to stay?"

"No, I'll be fine," Roy said quietly as he took another shot of scotch. He looked up almost as if he were looking through the ceiling toward heaven. "I know what I need to do."

"All right, but I'm just across the way if you need me. Don't do anything foolish though, you hear?" With that Greg walked out, gently closing the door.

On a perfect sunny Sunday morning in Los Angeles, a slight breeze made the leaves on the palm trees dance a slow, sensuous dance. Ikal had come back sometime during the night and had fallen asleep on the couch. Crushed beer cans lay strewn around him like crumpled unfinished love letters. Roy had taken the two cats in the bedroom with him and had fallen asleep in the midst of purring and the haze of scotch.

Roy opened his eyes and looked up at the ceiling. He held his hand to his mouth, and as his body jerked forward, he leaned over the edge of the bed and heaved in a bucket. He hung there, motionless, hearing the familiar sounds of Ikal preparing the large pot of espresso that they always shared. As the smell of coffee reached Roy's bedroom, the doorbell rang. Roy lifted his head and looked toward the closed bedroom door. Ikal never answered the door when someone knocked, never answered the phone when it rang; he was always afraid of the unknown. Roy still didn't move. If no one answered the door, it would all simply go away. But the bell just kept ringing and ringing. Finally, Roy lurched to his feet and staggered out of the bedroom. Ikal, pouring milk and sugar into two cups, looked at Roy, perplexed.

Roy opened the door and laughed nervously when he saw the two men. They didn't look anything like they do in the movies. Instead of suits and ties, they wore jeans and T-shirts. Flashing a badge, one of them stated in a steely, diplomatic tone, "We're from the Immigration and Naturalization Office. We're looking for Ikal Costa Nunes. We understand he is living here."

Roy turned to find Ikal looking at him with terror in his eyes. Roy tried to speak, attempting to tell the agents that there was no Ikal here. "Perhaps next door? I was angry, you see …" He blushed, made frantic meaningless gestures with his hands. "The scotch. It was too much!" Then he screamed, "I made a terrible mistake!"

The cups crashing on the floor made Roy jump. Ikal ran to the back door. The agents barreled through the door and chased after him, ordering him to stop as they pulled out their guns.

Roy clutched his chest again, trying to catch his breath. "There's been a mistake!" he wailed. "Please, there's been a mistake!" But before he knew it, Ikal was handcuffed and being escorted out. Roy followed them outside to a waiting van.

In the courtyard, Ikal, no longer struggling, gazed at the wilted impatiens. He turned toward Roy, eyes fixed on his, and said, "Who has made the hideous, the hurting, the insulting mistake of loving me, and must be punished for it. George and Martha, sad, sad, sad."

The officers looked confused.

"Te quiero mucho mi amor," were the last words Roy heard Ikal say.

Roy stood in silence as the van pulled away. Alone, he touched his own earlobe, slowly caressing it as Ikal had so often done. He looked up at Greg and Bert's windows and noticed Bert peering down at him. The old man looked shaken as he reached to open the window. But then he stopped midway, shook his head, closed his eyes, and drew the curtains closed.

Roy looked around as if it were the first time he'd ever been there, like someone searching for something but having forgotten what. He looked up toward the Hollywood sign, tears streaming down his face. "Words …" he whispered to himself, "that's all they were supposed to be."

Roy entered the apartment. He was about to close the door but stopped and left it ajar. In the kitchen, the mugs lay shattered on the floor. He walked to the couch, stepping over the empty beer cans, and sat holding the pillow that Ikal had slept on. In time his eyes fell upon Ikal's backpack tucked under the coffee table. He felt his pulse throb in his ears. He opened the backpack and found old copies of Penny Savers, real estate brochures featuring homes in Beverly Hills, a catalogue from the Los Angeles City College, a worn Spanish/English paperback dictionary, a tattered, dog-eared copy of *Who's Afraid of Virginia Woolf?* and, folded inside, an expired one-way ticket to Guadalajara. Lastly, a Hallmark card, the envelope bearing his name in Ikal's handwriting.

He looked around the empty apartment, seeming to wait for the music to swell and the words THE END to appear. He opened the card.

Do-Over

Deb stood at the grave site holding her breath, surrounded by an endless sea of flowers, unsure of what came next. It looks like the Brooklyn Botanic Gardens, she thought. The mourners, who only moments before had stood beside her mumbling words of comfort pledging that anything she needed was hers, had, with heads shaking and shoulders slumped, quickly made their way outside the gates of the cemetery, catching up to life and the living. A sudden wind encircled her. She felt herself being lifted. She let go, closed her eyes, and took a deep breath—and then it stopped. Just like that, she was alone. What the hell just happened? Deb thought, Is this for real?

Deb sat in her kitchen as the elevator of the prewar brick building clicked and buzzed making its way up and down the drafty shaft as tenants arrived home from work—some complaining about their jobs, some bragging about their kids and some hurrying to crack open that first can of beer of the night. The kitchen table was set for four but only one plate held remnants of a steak and salad. Next to it a soiled pasta bowl showed streaks of tomato sauce wiped clean by bread. She burped and looked around the empty table. "Excuse me," she said to no one. She walked over to the corner of the kitchen where the dog's water bowl sat, reached down, rinsed it, and filled it up once more with cool water. Placing it down again on the plastic placemat stamped with tiny blue paws, she whistled and waited, looking around for a moment. But Sammy didn't come. Returning to the kitchen counter she opened a bottle of pills, took one and then placed one pill inside each of the compartments of the pill box labeled with letters for each day of the week—happy to have found one at the Dollar Store that held enough pills for four weeks. She poured the rest into a coffee can already a quarter full with the tiny oval-shaped pills. She placed the can inside the refrigerator, in the back of the top shelf, behind four large bottles of ketchup, two large containers of mustard, two family-size jars of pickles, and a large bottle of soy sauce. "I'm never going to Costco again—what the hell am I going to do with all of this crap? Open up a diner?"

The cattail of the kitty clock swung slowly from side to side, wheezing. The hour dial, having fallen, sat somewhere inside the face of the clock. The minute dial struggled, clicking in place, picking up the rhythm of the cat's tail. Deb had not tried to repair the clock. She wanted to see how long it would keep going before it completely stopped. It was the only thing she had taken from Lena's apartment. Lena had been over the moon the day she spotted the clock at the Fort Greene Flea Market; it reminded her of her childhood. She didn't recall whose home it hung in, but it brought her warm memories of growing up in Carrol Gardens. Every night after dinner Lena would knock on the door and yell, "Time to exercise!" Then they'd take brisk walks along Prospect Park as cars whizzed by. Lena was the mother Deb wished she'd had. Her death had been so vicious, so senseless. Some sick lunatic pushed her on the train tracks as the train barreled into the station. She didn't stand a chance. The thought that kept coming back to Deb was whether she had died instantly or felt the pain of the wheels slicing her apart. She was sure she could ask someone, but was afraid of hearing what she already knew.

"Time to exercise," Deb whispered, walking to the living room and turning on the set. "Youtube, pilates—haven't seen this one." She sat, opening up a bag of Doritos, eating them one at the time, chewing slowly. "Now that looks like it hurts. If that cable snaps, she'll end up in Guam."

She touched her large belly that had become a guessing game for people walking by her, staring at it, trying to figure out if she had swallowed a basketball or if, perhaps, she was one of those freaks having kids way past their prime. "I'm not expecting," she would say under her breath, "it's just fat." She'd tried to cut down on the wine, the pasta, and cooking recipes copied from videos on Youtube made by cheerful unknown self-proclaimed chefs. She'd been unsuccessful. Every night she swore that it would change; the next day would be the day she'd start a healthy diet, and a morning workout. But in the morning the plan felt too ambitious, the motivation was not there. Then she'd look in the mirror feeling defeated. Maybe start slowly, a walk after dinner with the goal of going back to the gym and maybe even looking into Jenny Craig. That was the plan she'd ultimately decide upon and hope, one day to start—when she felt better.

This girl is limber. I give her that, she thought as she popped another Dorito into her mouth. She laughed. "Junior's gotta see this," she said as she reached for the receiver. She picked it up and put it to her ear. The harsh buzzing of the dial tone and the sudden wailing from the siren of an ambulance speeding by the building jolted her back to reality. "Goddamn it! Why does this keep happening? Son of a bitch!" She slammed the phone down. "Sammy!" she yelled. "Let's go to bed. I've had enough." She looked around. "Oh, damn, —yeah, time to go to bed."

It was the same dream every night.

Their favorite song, "Love is in the Air," plays on the radio, he comes in, kisses her on the cheek, tastes the tomato sauce with pork ribs that's been simmering adagio, adagio, for over two hours, and grins, "The best!" He wraps his rough, calloused hands around her face, and says "I love you!"

He heads toward the bathroom and calls out, "I can't wait to eat—fresh fettuccine from Pastosa, I hope? Maybe a quickie on the fire escape before dinner after my shower?" He winks. She reaches out to embrace him, he is gone.

It was morning—again. No need to look at the clock; Deb knew the time: 4:30 AM. She reached over to the other side of the bed and touched the pillow, as she always did every morning. All she felt was the cold sheet still pulled tight, untouched. Deb still hadn't opened her eyes, but she knew she was smiling.

She laid still as she always did, desperate for sleep to return so she could dream of him and maybe this time, touch him. But when sleep refused to take her back to her dream, she wished for death. Then everything would be right. She waited, but nothing happened. Instead, she felt her lower back struggling to keep flat against the mattress. "Get up!" The voice in her head screamed. The charley horse was coming, she knew it instinctively.

Goddamn it! She thought, I didn't drink enough water last night! As her calf began its contraction, she bolted out of the bed careful not to lose her balance as she tried to extend her leg to prevent the muscle from cramping. God knew she could take pain, but Deb found it unbearable so early in the morning along with everything else she had to deal with. She willed it away and then hesitantly placed her weight on the leg. It was gone.

Now all she could hear was her own breathing. It was always too quiet this time of the morning—she hated that. She tapped her finger on the nightstand, making sure she'd not gone deaf. Thankfully it was Thursday, garbage pick-up. She could already hear the trucks, faint sounds of brakes screeching every few feet, then after a beat or two, the sound of their bowels expanding, gorging themselves on left-over rotting meat and the remains of things no longer wanted or needed.

Deb made her way to the bathroom and flipped the light switch on the side of the medicine cabinet. She preferred yellow lightbulbs in the fixture above the mirror, the kind people use outdoors to keep bugs away. They made her look jaundiced but she didn't care; at that time of the morning, she found the light to be softer, kinder to her complexion and most importantly, forgiving of all the blemishes and lines on her face. The inevitable aging process had covertly set itself in motion on a day when she had not been looking. She stared hard in the mirror asking the same question she had asked countless times before: "Where did the time go? How can I still have the needs of a young woman, but look like somebody's grandmother?"

Every morning she'd scrutinize her reflection like an archeologist studying an artifact just dug up, carefully scrubbing it clean of the dried mud concealing its original beauty. The skin of her eyelids had given away to gravity, now looking much like a tired and sad hound dog. Her eyebrows, once commanding, able to convey sultriness by simply rising up, were now tiny gardens with annoying little weeds popping up faster than she could get rid of them. As soon as she plucked them, they were back the next morning. Her hair had begun thinning after it all happened and now what was left were patches here and there that her hairdresser carefully manipulated and sculpted into place in an attempt to fool her and those who looked at her into believing that she still had a good head of hair. But ultimately looking as if she was wearing a helmet made of spider webs. She had no idea why she even cared at this point—was vanity something she should be concerned about? But she wouldn't allow anyone to ridicule her. Not even Junior, her best friend. "Fuck you! I'm not going through chemo! It's just a bad hair day," she yelled at Junior, the only person that had not allowed her to feel sorry for herself. "Did I say anything to you when you got sick and looked like a skeleton with bulging eyes?"

"That's beyond harsh, you bitch!" Junior said angrily. Both were fuming and then, unable to contain themselves, began to laugh until their sides hurt. They'd embraced and held one another until the laughter turned to tears. Deb loved him. He hadn't bounced back that last time and then he was gone. It shouldn't have happened, not at this stage of the game, thought Deb, not after all the fear. There was so much more hope now. Not like before.

Every day, she still expected her front door to open and for Junior to come in, heading straight to the kitchen to grab a cup of coffee, never taking a breath as he spilled gossip from around the building. He had been the only one that could, at times, make her feel like she was still alive. Yeah, she thought, as she had dozens of times, a real damn shame he didn't bounce back that last time.

And then she heard the voice in her head, "I want a do-over! I want a do-over! I WANT A DO-OVER!" She shook her head to make it go away. Deb felt her legs begin to tremble. She held on to the sides of the vanity, took a deep breath, and looked around for the toothpaste. She saw it where she had left it after having squeezed every last bit of it the day before. She had intended on buying it, but forgot to do it like always. Why? Why had it always been a problem to remember to buy toothpaste? Did she think it would last forever? She unrolled the tube and pressed and pulled back and forth on the side of the sink hoping that a tiny nurdle of toothpaste would make its way out. It didn't, so she took the toothbrush and inserted as many bristles as she could inside the tip of the tube. She got just enough to at least brush her teeth, rinse, and spit. Deb reached for the shower curtain, stepped in and closed her eyes, turned the faucet on and pulled the diverter. The water came out cold and she let out a scream that lasted until the water turned warm and then hot. The shock of the cold water confirmed that she was still alive.

"Just barely," she heard someone say.

"There it is again! That goddamned voice!" she said shaking her head. With her eyes shut tight she lathered, trying to avoid feeling her body and then quickly rinsed. She reached for the robe she'd taken from the Blue Moon Hotel in Montego Bay. Its sleeves and belt were frayed, but it helped bring the memories back of that unforgettable week in Jamaica with Johnny Boy, in a private bungalow on the beach, treated like royalty and feeling like Gods—regardless of the fact that they were spending the last of their savings and didn't know how they would pay their rent that month. She wrapped the robe a little tighter around her and then sat on the side of the bed. Looking at the framed photos on the dresser and without emotion, she said, "Good morning, everyone." She smiled. "Everyone is dead," she said and covered her mouth with her hand but she didn't cry.

Deb leaned back on Johnny's side of the bed and placed her head on his pillow. She untied her robe. At first, she looked toward the ceiling and then she gazed down, toward her naked body; she scanned it without stopping to focus on any one part, but couldn't help but notice that her breasts were not where they were supposed to be. They had fallen to the sides of her body, totally relaxed, seeming to want to snuggle under the crooks of her armpits. It all started going to shit that awful day, she thought, in Neiman Marcus. She could never forget it. It was around the time she'd begun putting on an extra couple of pounds, "More of you to love," Johnny Boy had murmured in her ear thrusting from behind. Then why wouldn't he look in her eyes as he made love to her? She had begun to worry. Her period had stopped. She knew where she was heading—menopause. She could never forget her mother telling her about her Aunt Rita back in Italy and how she would stand on the balcony lifting her blouse to show her breasts to the men coming back from the fields. That's how Zia dealt with her change of life but Deb couldn't face it with such rebellious gusto. That day at Neiman's she had decided to buy a new outfit, something colorful, sexy. But she was feeling… not right—something was off. It started slowly, nudging her, making itself known: "I'm here! Wanna play?" She knew there was no stopping it, she knew it as soon as it reared its ugly head. That overwhelming sense of total loss of control. And if that wasn't enough, she also had to pee. It began at the base of her neck, an intense heat climbing, like a boiler trying to hit 90 degrees to satisfy the thermostat's demand. That all-consuming heat quickly rising like a swarm of ants engulfing the body of a dead water-bug. She was suddenly damp; then she was soaked. The sweat seeped through her clothes as her body demanded to be released from the suffocating heat. She removed her coat and scarf, but it was not enough. Her face flushed, her eyes went blood shot like a human transforming into a werewolf. She no longer cared and standing between ladies' petite lingerie and the full-figured lady section with its many colorful bellowing tent-like dresses, she removed her sweater. Still that searing heat that punishes women between the end of their fertile period and death (but that men are spared from never having a clue to what hell feels like) exploded throughout her body and in desperation she removed her slacks in an attempt to escape being crisped, until the demon finally released her. Then as she laid in her bra and panties on the cool, vinyl tiles on the third floor of Neiman Marcus, she smiled, unconcerned by the approaching security guards and the group of people that encircled her, some amused, some shocked and some women even commiserating while pleading within that it would never happen to them. She now laughed at the memory of that day because she couldn't cry—the meds made sure of that.

Deb made her bed, dressed, changed the water in the bowl for Sammy, and made an espresso. Every day she thought that the next day would be better. She'd been told as much by so many people that it would be. She looked at the coffee table brimming with books about healing after losing loved ones, the pamphlets about grief, the schedules for support groups that she had attended and had left, unable to cleanse herself of the despair that clung to her. And every day she would ask, "Now what?" Everywhere she went, Johnny was there.

"What can I get you today?" a smiling deli clerk asked.

"Quarter pound of ham, a quarter of soppressatta and a

quarter of provolone, everything sliced paper-thin," Deb said, looking at the dozen just-made mozzarella balls on the counter. A hand reached over her shoulder, taking one from the tray. Suddenly she could smell Johnny Boy's cologne. She closed her eyes inhaling the scent swaddling her. She trembled, took a breath and turned around. The man was already down an aisle toward the exit. "Johnny?" she whispered. She looked at the mozzarella. She wanted to cry but instead she began laughing as she picked one up taking a closer look, examining it.

The deli clerk smiled uncertainly.

Her laughter became louder, harsher. A woman waiting to be served took a few steps back. The clerk continued slicing furiously, trying to get the order done as quickly as possible. He yelled over his shoulder toward the woman, "I'll be with you in a moment, ma'am." But she was gone.

By now Deb's laughter had become maniacal, sounding more like the howls of an animal being tortured in a trap. The deli clerk quickly wrapped and priced the order and with his arm extended placed it on the counter and stepped back. In a shaky voice, he said, "It's ready."

Deb's laughter instantly stopped. "Thanks," she said as she picked up the cold cuts. "Great job, appreciate it." The young man just stood there with a frightened smile watching her as she walked away. She knew everyone thought her crazy, but she didn't care. It was what she called, losing-her-shit-moments, and what she sometimes needed to do to make it through the day.

"Hey doll, I'll be working late again tonight, gotta be up

early, set the alarm for me? 4:30? I always forget! Oh, and by the way, you think you could pick up some toothpaste? We're scraping the bottom of the barrel here." Those were the last words she'd ever heard Johnny Boy say. In the beginning she could hear his voice in her head; loud, clear, indestructible. "I'll see you later doll!" But as time went by his voice became dimmer, smaller and distant like the faintness of a last echo before complete silence.

The prescriptions for antidepressants and anti-anxiety pills prescribed by the twenty-nine-year-old psychiatrist, whose name was Dr. Dickerson, but whom she referred to as Dr. Dick, were always renewed even before he asked how she was doing. Deb had coaxed the young man to up the quantity so she'd have a back-up. "Just in case you are on vacation or something," she said sweetly, looking somewhere above his head in an attempt to avoid his eyes.

"This is a powerful drug, remember, no alcohol," Dick would warn while squinting his eyes for effect. He had fashioned himself after a Sigmund Freud whose preference was rap rather than classical music. Dr. Dick's full beard, round glasses and severe, almost menacing gaze were strangely incongruous to his baggy pants, loose, oversized t-shirts and the white, untied Adidas sneakers he wore. "Do you feel these medications are working for you?" he would ask while reassuring her that he understood what she was going through though he couldn't possibly have had any clue.

"Yes," she'd say, "the pills are working. At least I don't cry anymore." And then he'd nod making a note on his pad signaling that their time together was over.

Dr. Dick kept her medicated while her therapist tried to help her cope with her day-to-day. "Do you have thoughts of suicide?" was the first thing the therapist would always ask. Deb could never remember her name. She was just out of school. Pretty, thin, with a waist that reminded Deb of a Barbie doll. She was blonde, with blue eyes that darted around the room looking at everything except for Deb's eyes. At their first session, Deb needed to open up to someone, just to hear herself say the words. She had begun to think that it all had been her imagination and she was stuck in a nightmare. Who knows, she had thought, maybe I'm being a bit of a bitch, maybe Barbie can help.

"Please go ahead," said Barbie. "Tell me what's on your mind."

"Okay," Deb began, still skeptical. "My best friend, who had been in my life since we were in kindergarten, who I shared all my secrets with, who understood me better than I understand myself, died in my arms, suffocating on his own vomit. And there was nothing I could do to help him except to look at that empty, faraway look in his eyes until he was gone."

"I'm so sorry," Barbie said, lowering her voice just so. "Death is a difficult thing to deal with. I can," Deb interrupted her.

"There's more," Deb stated. "My next-door neighbor was sliced and diced by a subway car because someone woke up that morning on the wrong side of the bed and since it was going to be a shitty day, why not push someone in front of a train just for shits and giggles?"

"Oh my," the young therapist almost shrieked. "That's horrible! Maybe we can discuss how these losses have —"

"There's more," Deb said.

"More?" The young woman looked startled.

"My husband was like no other man I'd ever known. He is gone. When he told me I love you, I not only heard the words but felt that love in every bone in my body. I believed him. He cared for me so much that he worked three jobs to save for a down payment on a little place on Staten Island, not our favorite borough but it was what we could afford. 'Brooklyn is just a bridge away, we can come back anytime,' he'd say." Deb paused; the therapist didn't say anything; she just sat there. Deb didn't continue until the young girl's face was directly facing Deb's looking into her eyes. "That morning was windy. He should not have not gone up that skeleton of a building. The crane swayed back and forth, in and out of the low clouds, picking up momentum until one huge gust of wind swung the girder on the cable. It snapped from the hoist and came down, smashing the construction elevator. The cab gave away, barreling down." Deb covered her eyes as if wanting the image to disappear from her mind. "He must have been terrified. He had to know he was about to die, there, alone, without one last kiss."

At some point the therapist had taken a Kleenex out of the box next to Deb and was drying her eyes. Deb understood it was too much for Barbie to hear—probably her greatest loss had been losing a cat in ninth grade. She couldn't deal with the pain that she was being served on a silver platter so Deb decided to hold back telling her about Sammy going to the vet for a routine teeth cleaning and never waking up from the anesthesia. She was sure Barbie would have had a total collapse receiving that news.

They'd had only a few sessions when one day, after listening to Barbie explaining how grief comes and goes and that every day is a new day, Deb told her that her advice and keen observations had already helped her so much, she felt that she could move on, that she could now deal with her anxiety and depression. She thanked her and said that it may be time to try managing on her own. Barbie quickly agreed to end their sessions, but insisted that Deb see Dr. Dick so that he could evaluate her medication intake. Deb retreated backwards out the door, genuflecting, thanking her. As the door closed behind her, Deb gave it the middle finger.

Deb now sat at the kitchen table wiping invisible dust away with her bare hand while her finger scratched a burnt cigarette mark made by someone playing poker many Thursdays ago as life buzzed around unconcerned with its own vulnerability. The kitty clock took a last gasp. It rattled and then it was silent. The stillness made the universe pause for a deafening moment before continuing its eternal journey. "That's it! I'm done," she yelled, grabbing her purse and walking out of the apartment, slamming the door with such vehemence, the sound of it echoed throughout the building.

Deb hurried down Fourth Ave as the express Q train rumbled below. She looked toward the Williamsburg Savings

Bank Tower, once the tallest building in Brooklyn but now surrounded by skyscrapers, some completed, some about to be, and others quickly rising toward the sky attempting to surpass one another. Everything has changed, Deb thought, I don't recognize my world anymore.

She reached CVS on the corner of Fourth and Baltic, the last of its kind—it had a parking lot. Deb reached for a cart from the stacked line—it was stuck. She pulled and pulled and then began hitting it with her purse. "What the fuck!!! Did you weld these things together?" Then, she saw one of the cart collectors walk toward her. Without saying a word, he pulled the cart while lifting the one in the front. It gave way without the slightest bit of resistance. He rolled it to Deb. "What can I say," she mumbled, "you've got that magic touch! Thanks."

Deb went through each aisle, tossing in toothpaste, new tweezers, a face mask, hot wax for the legs, nail polish, mascara, foundation, eyeliner, lipstick, moisturizers for every part of the body and then headed to the cashier. As she waited in line, she took inventory of the products in the cart. She shook her head and smiled. I should treat myself, she thought. At the register, instead of placing the items on her counter, she said, "I'm sorry, I'll pay for the restocking. I'll just take the toothpaste."

The cashier rolled her eyes, annoyed. She looked over at the cart and scanned the toothpaste. "Sure, no problem. We don't charge for restocking." She dismissed Deb's offer with a mocking smile. "That will be four seventy-nine. Need a receipt?"

Deb stood there for a second, wanting to rip the girl's head off her shoulders, but instead said, "Nah, you keep it. Something to remember me by." She headed toward the exit and as the doors slid open, she heard a faint, "Crazy bitch!" coming from the general direction of the cashier. Deb laughed—meaning it.

She crossed Flatbush and headed south to 7th Ave. She reached Suzy's Beauty Salon & Spa. She walked in and while still holding the door open, she yelled, "Bitches! I'm back! Not a word about my fat ass! Full treatment today, Brazilian wax, legs, facial, make-up, full body massage—someone who can handle all of this!"

Suzy, standing in the corner with her hands in a sink scrubbing someone's scalp, laughed and said, "Sure D! Anything for my girl! We're doing hair too?"

"Nope," replied Deb, "I've discovered turbans, like Lana Turner wore back in the day! With the right kind of make-up, I'll look stunning! Who needs hair?"

"What's the special occasion?" Suzy asked teasingly.

"Oh, I'm meeting some very nice people that I haven't seen in a long time."

Suzy went over to Deb and took her hand. "I'm so happy to see you back! Missed you, you nut! Glad you are moving on—life needs to go on." She hugged her as Deb's entire body stiffened.

After getting the royal treatment and hearing the latest neighborhood gossip, she paid, said her goodbyes, promising to be back soon, and headed toward the door. She stopped at one of the mirrors. She scanned herself from top to bottom. She tilted her head. "Hah!" she uttered and walked out.

On her way home, Deb walked by Giuseppina's on 6th and 21st Street. She paused, delighting in the scent of pizza cooking in the wood fired oven. The place had been owned by the same family since 1932. Deb had always pictured them cooking in the kitchen, laughing and patting each other on the back. One for the road, she thought, walking in and heading straight to her favorite table in the back corner so she would have a view of the entire place. She ordered a small margherita pizza with capers and olives and a carafe of the house wine. She had no choice but to order the house red—Giuseppina's never served any other wine. For years Deb was convinced it was made in the basement by Giuseppina's Uncle Louie.

As the order was being prepared, she looked around at the other tables, couples looking down at their phones, some, even as they were taking a bite of their pizza or sipping on their wine, young parents wrestling their kids back down on their high chairs scolding them, "Is this the way to behave? How many times do we have to have this conversation? We discussed this at length before leaving the house." An older couple eating their meal silently looked on, shaking their heads, disapprovingly.

Deb had already downed two of the four glasses of wine the carafe held when the waiter arrived with her pizza. "What happened here?" she said. "People used to laugh, sing and enjoy themselves. It looks like a reunion of the young, old and the miserable!"

"Couldn't agree with you more," said the waiter. "Once real estate prices around here went through the roof, the old timers were pushed out and these nuts showed up. If I ever acted like these kids in a restaurant or any other place for that matter, my father would have knocked my ass into next week and back. By the way, the wine is on me. I heard. It sucks. It's been a very long time but it's good to see you back. Next time maybe we can share a glass of wine?" He walked away. Deb sat, looking down at her food, thinking back to a time when she'd be surrounded by her friends, by the love of her life. She slowly ate the pizza and each bite brought back more and more memories. She sat there until her check arrived. "You be good now, I was really happy to see you," the waiter said as he squeezed her hand. His touch was warm. It felt strange. It had been so long. She thought she was almost going to cry but instead grabbed the check, found loose cash inside her purse, threw it on the table and walked out.

The air was crisp, cool, smelling of an early Spring. Deb's head pleasantly spinning having finished the carafe of wine. Soon the lilac bushes will bloom, she thought. Every year, she'd drag Johnny Boy to the Brooklyn Botanic Gardens. She smiled, suddenly feeling lighter than she had in a long time. And she began to hum their song. When she arrived at her go-to liquor store, she found herself standing in front of a newly opened nail salon instead. Out loud she said, "Christ, I really have been out of the loop. What's with all the nail salons?!"

She then spotted a small storefront across the street with a sign that read SIP. Outside a double-sided blackboard read,

A Day Without Wine is a Day Without Love. Catchy, Deb thought. She walked in and to no one in particular announced, "Like the sign! Do you also sell booze?"

She walked out holding one of those bags made of recycled materials with inserts for bottles: a bottle of gin for her, single malt scotch for Johnny Boy and Vodka for her besties.

Deb unlocked the front door of the apartment, stepped in and stood in the silence. I'm really going through with it, she thought as her hand gripped the door knob tightly. Slowly, she closed the door, but didn't lock it. In the kitchen, she tried organizing what she needed, but found herself meandering, her hands trembling as she opened the refrigerator to reach for the coffee can. She shook it—the pills making a sound like that of a baby's rattle. After about an hour, she finally assembled what she needed. Along with Sammy's bowl she brought everything to her bedroom. She placed the bowl on the left side of the bed, where she slept. She arranged a bucket of ice and the bottles of gin, vodka and scotch near the three glasses she had placed in front of the photographs. She opened the can and lined the pills along the entire edge of the dresser. This should take care of business, she thought.

From her closet she pulled out a pink babydoll negligee and a white sheer lounging gown she'd bought one Valentine's Day to surprise Johnny Boy. She undressed. God, I hope it fits, she thought, uncertain. Holding her breath, she draped the babydoll on and slipped into the gown. Both were a bit snug but they fit. She stood there touching her body; she felt it tingle, smooth, warm, plump and sensuous, smelling of lavender.

In the bathroom, she turned on the switch to the recessed ceiling lights and adjusted her eyes to the harsh brightness of the bulbs. She took the new tube of toothpaste and vigorously brushed her teeth. She caressed her face with both hands, pulling back the skin of her neck. Her make-up had been painted on with loving care, with importance, with meaning, knowing that it was for a very special occasion. The light blue eye shadow, the black thin liner, the concealer under her eyes, the delicately sculpted lashes and perfectly shaped eyebrows brought vibrancy to her eyes and face. Her skin glowed—gold specs in the face powder sparkling and bouncing as she moved her face in slow motion like a model on a television commercial selling face cream. She was renewed. She pulled a ready-made silver turban over her head. She paused, smiled and said, "Not bad for a crazy, over the hill, depressed old broad!"

Satisfied she walked into the bedroom and poured the drinks. "Scotch, one ice for my love, vodka straight up for Junior and for you Lena, vodka tonic. And for me? Gin and tonic, no ice!" Deb felt elated. She popped a pill in her mouth and downed the scotch. She took a second and downed the vodka. She shivered. She could feel her heart racing. She downed the gin and tonic and reached for another pill, but stopped. Instead, she began swaying and singing, "Love is in the air, every time I look at you. Love is in the air…." She mixed another gin and tonic and continued singing, closing her eyes as moments of joy flashed in her mind: birthdays, dinners with everyone yelling around the table, holidays with lots of gifts, watching the fireworks, strong arms holding her on the Brooklyn

Bridge, making love on the roof, back rubs, kisses in the shower, surprise parties, hugs that felt as if they would go on forever and love, so much love. And then she heard the voice in her head, "Do-over! Do-over! Do-over!"

"But I'm going now," Deb said.

"Not yet, first, the do-over," she heard the voice say again, and then she crashed on the bed as memories faded into oblivion.

Deb opened her eyes. She didn't know where she was. Thirsty. Mouth dry. Something in her throat. She tried to swallow. Her body was frozen. Everything was spinning. She laid there staring at the ceiling feeling nothing. "Oh my god! Am I dead?" she said. And then she cocked her head from side to side looking around the room. "I'm not dead? What the fuck!" she screamed, "I'm not dead! I'm not dead!" she repeated, confused as she reached for the alarm clock. Her blurry eyes focused on the time. "8:30? What the hell is going on here? 8:30?" She looked at the photographs on the dresser. Something was different about them. The smiles on their faces weren't *within* the photographs, they were smiling *at* her. She felt comforted, peaceful, protected by arms holding her tight. Deb felt all their love washing over her as she heard Johnny Boy say, "I love you."

Then in a whisper Deb said, "It's not 4:30."

She heard voices coming from outside: laughter, energetic vibrant laughter and shrieks from children going to school.

She reached over to the other side of the bed and put her hand on the pillow. What now? What do I do now? she thought.

"Do-over," she heard herself say.

Cocoon

Our eyes locked as I grabbed a slice of pizza from Nunzio's Pizza, across from the main building of Baruch City College. It was packed as always, a goldmine. Should I walk over? I thought, say something? But I could never walk up to a girl. My fear, fueled by inexperience, self-doubt, and ignorance, always took over. I was paralyzed. So, I just stood there. Instead, she made her way through the crowd of students waiting in line for their slice of heaven. "Excuse me, excuse me," she said quite loudly. Suddenly stalled by a group on non-movers she firmly announced, "I said excuse me! Now move out of my way!" The sea parted, no one saying a word. She walked up to me as I was taking my first bite of the steaming hot pizza. Just like that! Without hesitation and with a confidence I had never seen in anyone, especially myself. "We need to connect. I feel we have something to share. I knew I would meet you today! What's your sign?" She said as she took the change from the counter and slid it into my coat pocket.

I winced as the scalding mozzarella cheese welded to the upper palate of my mouth. My eyes widened. I felt huge tears flooding my eyes. I swallowed, in a gulp, the mouthful of dough, sauce and cheese I had bitten into, trying to assess what degree of burn I had caused to the roof of my mouth.

"Everything okay?" she asked, oblivious to the fact that I was hopping from the pain as tiny skin flakes peeled off in my mouth.

All I could get out was a, "Huh," while forcing a smile as the tears slid down the sides of my eyes. There was still no reaction from her.

"I'm Sarah, Sarah Roche," she announced almost as if I should know who she was.

"Saverio Tumino, nice to meet you," I said wondering whether she even wanted to know.

She didn't look like other girls. She wore men's clothing—cargo pants that were way too big for her, held up by three braided men's ties of various stripes and colors, a gray t-shirt emblazoned with a yellow middle finger, a red plaid shirt and a man's wool blazer with elbow patches that looked like a large coat on her. This eclectic ensemble looked as if it hadn't been cleaned in a while. Her blonde hair drooped down around her shoulders like overcooked spaghetti, limp, lifeless. It wasn't shiny, it looked matted in places, like you couldn't run your fingers through it. I couldn't help but think of the many old homeless women pushing shopping carts up and down Broadway. But, underneath this bizarre getup I could tell there was a truly beautiful young woman. Her skin was rosy and delicate tiny freckles dotted her cheeks. She had sparkling blue eyes, and her pupils seemed to be breathing. They were hypnotizing me; they knew with total certainty what they wanted, and would, unequivocally possess it.

"I guess a Taurus? That's April, right?" I said, having somehow regained my composure.

"A bull, I knew it. You're strong and determined, I think we'll get along just fine. I'm a Libra. I am very balanced—most of the time, when I'm not... I can become pretty crazy." She said winking. I blushed. It was the first time anyone had referred to me as strong and determined or winked at me.

"Come—walk with me," she said, taking hold of my arm and leading me down Broadway as I tossed the rest of the pizza in a garbage basket. I had class in a half an hour, but that didn't seem to stop me from being led away. It felt like the most natural thing in the world to do. I never deviated from the road I was on, never. I had been kept in a cocoon by my parents all my life and had not been allowed out, it was never the right time. I didn't understand anything about life or what it meant to have fun. I had never had a girlfriend or known what it felt to be close to a girl. At twenty my experiences had been created in my imagination and brought to life while in the shower.

"I attend NYU," she said, just a fact, without the slightest hint of superiority. "I have a lot of friends at Baruch, that's why I like hanging out here." I was smitten and jealous at the same time, though I would never admit it, even to myself. I mentioned that I had really wanted to go to NYU. I didn't want her to think I wouldn't have been accepted based on my grades and SAT score, so I didn't lie, which I grew up being told was the best thing I could do. "My family couldn't afford it." I blurted out.

"NYU isn't anything special. A bunch of spoiled rich kids

with no idea of what the world really has in store for them," she said brushing it away like someone waving away an annoying gnat from her ear. I guess it was her way of making me feel better about attending a city college.

"Well, we could if it wasn't for the house being built in Sicily," I said, somewhat sheepishly. Sarah looked intrigued.

"I love Italy! Went there in my senior year of high school. I fell in love. The food! The history! Alessandro! The bell-hop at our hotel, handsome beyond words—he insisted that he had fallen in love the moment he saw me. I vowed the same, I fibbed. It wasn't love but I couldn't deny he had amazing skills. The magic lasted an entire five days. He swore he would follow me to the States, but of course didn't. I knew he wouldn't," she said, laughing. "Love at first sight is a silly concept and not very realistic, don't you agree?"

I nodded but said nothing. I had never had an Italian adventure. Every summer we'd go back to the small Sicilian town where my parents were born. It was dismal: a piazza with a non-working fountain, old men with their heads resting on folded hands propped up by their canes sitting silently at the only café in town, and a massive church whose bell seemed to be constantly tolling, and nothing else. I hated that place. We never made friends because there were no friends to make; most of the younger families had moved away. As soon as the school year was over, we would head to this desolate place. My father joined us in August to work on the house that he swore we would eventually return to live in once he felt we had enough money to sustain us while he built up his business. It was surrounded by land packed with fruit and olive trees. It didn't rain much but the wind storms were relentless. The dry air covered your skin in a veil of dust that made you look like a zombie in a horror movie. I prayed we'd never have enough money to move there.

Sarah turned down Fifth Avenue and headed south, toward Washington Square Park. I followed. Whenever I was in Manhattan, I found myself running along with everyone else, zigzagging in and out of crowds so as not to be in anyone's way. I just kind of followed along with the crowd. Sarah, however, meandered. There was no need to duck out of people's paths because they were the ones to move aside as she strolled along. Now and then she'd stop at a stand selling cheap jewelry, picking up a pair of earrings, holding them, and then dismissing them by tossing them back with a frown. At a grocery store fruit stand, she picked up an apple, took a few bites and pocketed the remainder. I stood there for a moment, then ran in to pay for it— she had probably forgotten to, I figured. It was as if the city was her playpen and everything in it belonged to her. She spoke to me like she had known me forever, and she didn't sugarcoat anything, "So much of this life sucks!" she'd inject here and there. She spoke with an authority unknown to me. She didn't hold back. She never second guessed herself. She knew it was so, even if it may not have been. I was the total opposite when it came to expressing my opinions: I was never sure anyone would find them convincing or even cared enough to listen.

Sarah told me all about herself and weirdly she didn't ask

too many questions of me. She grew up in Millburn, New Jersey, a very affluent area she described as being full of "rich assholes," and attended some of the best private schools "money could buy," she hissed in a disgusted tone. Her father was a successful attorney, "an ambulance chaser, a real peach of a man," she said sarcastically. In winter when Sarah's parents got tired of the cold weather in New York, they would pick up and go to the Bahamas.

The only traveling my parents did in the winter was when my mom guilted my father into taking a walk around the block at Christmas time to look at the neighbors' decorations.

She was a theatre major, minoring in women's studies. She shopped for secondhand clothes at the Thrift Boutique on Broadway and East 8th Street and only ate vegetables. She said that the only right thing to do for the planet was to be a vegetarian, and that is what she had chosen to be. "You should consider doing the same," she suggested with just the right amount of command in her voice to make me seriously consider doing it, out of fear? The first time I reached for my smokes, Kool Menthols, Sarah looked at me quizzically and with a nod toward the cigarette I was about to place in my mouth said, "You really hate yourself, don't you?"

"I know, they are bad for you, some say," I mumbled not sharing that it was the only vice my father approved of—men smoked. "I've been meaning to quit," I said.

"Try now. Don't smoke around me, it's that simple," she said as I put the cigarette back in its box.

Smoking wasn't the only thing that Sarah disapproved

of; she loathed perfumes, colognes of any kind, and even underarm deodorants, preferring "the natural scents that the body produced." She despised women who shaved their armpits, something she had in common with my mom; only loose women did that.

We finally arrived at Washington Square Park. I had promised my parents that I would never go anywhere in the city except to class, the library and then back home by subway—back to our safe neighborhood of Gravesend, in Brooklyn, a world unto its own, one stop from Coney Island, the last stop on the B subway train. Gravesend was a neighborhood of Italian-American families stuck in a time warp, everyone believing what they had been taught by strict parents, even stricter grandparents, and, of course, the church. It was where I grew up, slowly being basted in old customs, old ideas, and preconceived prejudices that one day would all involuntarily bleed out of me unless I could somehow find a way of exorcizing myself of them.

Sarah pointed to a bench closest in the center of the park so we could sit and study people walking by. "The answers to all our questions are here—watch, absorb, learn," she said as if revealing a most coveted secret. I couldn't imagine that all the answers I was looking for in life were in a park littered with garbage and passed out drunks, but I followed anyway. So, I just sat there, with this strange and beautiful girl waiting for her to share some wisdom, something I could take and run with, but then, she was suddenly quiet, still, so I sat there, next to her, in her stillness, and didn't utter a word—it's what

I thought she would have wanted me to do.

Weeks went by. We'd meet at Washington Square Park, sit on a bench, and I would listen to Sarah's diatribe about all that was wrong with her family. Her exhaustion and frustration, she explained, came from having grown up in a family of connivers, cold manipulators who never took into consideration anyone's feelings, especially their children. If she could, she would run away and never see them again. She wanted a wholesome life, a life based on self-respect. She wanted to contribute in a way that was mutually beneficial for herself and mankind, that was her goal. Every now and then, when I could muster the courage, I'd reach for her hand, and if she didn't pull away, I figured it was okay to hold it; she'd be still for a moment, and I'd gently pat it like the caretaker of a mental patient trying to keep her from imploding. I liked Sarah a lot, but I wasn't sure what it was she wanted or needed from me. Often times she would look at me and caress my face and then tell me how much I remind her of her bellhop back in Positano.

Sarah fought a stutter when she spoke of her parents. There was a bitterness in her voice that seemed to be veiling a sadness, a disappointment—her eyes cast down. Was it shame? "My father makes money from other people's pain and suffering while my mother is a pathetic housewife who spends most of her time taking *tennis lessons*." She spoke these words slowly, injecting as much sarcasm as the voice permits. "My mother," Sarah continued, "drinks martinis for lunch with her girlfriends and ends up passing out cold at seven just before dinner." Shaking her head, she repeated over and over, "That will never be me! Never! That will never be me!" I didn't think someone would talk about their personal life like that to a total stranger. But Sarah had no problem doing so.

She also had a very particular way of talking at me—not to me—something she shared with my parents. She knew more than I did in just about anything and that was probably true, and my parents had lived a lot longer than me so they came with more experience, but I don't recall any one of them ever asking, "What do you think, Saverio?" especially my father. He didn't simply talk like most people; he was always loud and threatening, which ultimately became his normal speaking voice. Whatever he said sounded like a command, even a simple hello. I had been brought up to fear him. Fear was something you needed to feel so that respect could be shown—that was my father's upbringing and now mine, and my sisters'.

My father never smiled. At least he never smiled at us. A nod of the head was his way to show approval, whether it was directed at us for having brought home a good report card or toward my mother for his approval of her cooking. If he didn't like something you did, he'd just stare you down until you cried. If he didn't particularly like the pasta sauce or the way a piece of meat was cooked, he'd push the plate away from him and ask for bread and cheese. My mother would put her fork down, get up, get the cheese, slice the bread, arrange it on a plate and place it in front of him. She would then rub the top of his hand gently with one finger, he'd look up, and she would smile apologetically. That was respect.

Sarah couldn't wait to be out on her own. A totally foreign

concept where I was concerned. In my family, you left when you either married or died. Sarah had her own studio apartment in the Village.

"Wow!" I said, "That's fantastic! I hear the rents around there are pretty steep," I said wanting to know how she was paying for the place.

"It's not a rental, they bought it as a pied-a-terre." Her eyes avoided mine. "My mother convinced my father to let me live there while I attend university." The tone of her voice was almost sweet. It didn't last. "My father is livid that now he can't use it for his trysts and has to go to hotels," she said loudly as she mimed vomiting.

Trysts? I wanted to ask how she knew about that, but thought it would be better to let that one go.

"My father pays for everything. It's his way to absolve himself of his sins," she said picking up a leaf and dissecting it trying to leave its skeleton whole. "That's the least he can do," she continued, her voice small and distant. But then she almost yelled, "The fucker missed every recital and play I was ever in and didn't even attend my high school graduation. I loathe him. He's everything that is wrong in this world," she said, with such anger and disgust that I wondered why she would even still be speaking to him.

One day in the park, in the middle of ranting about something, she invited me—or rather ordered me, over to her place. "You have time, right?" she said, knowing that I had four hours between classes on Tuesdays. "Something different instead of sitting here being shat on by pigeons."

Fear washed over me. I didn't understand why, but I was scared. Did she sense it? "It'll be chill. We can just hang out," she said, winking at me.

"Sure, of course, why not, of course, chill, I like hanging out," I stammered like a complete idiot.

I didn't sleep that night. I just kept trying to picture her place. Would she make me lunch? Did she have cake like my mom always had for company? Would she finally ask me about my life? Would she ask me who I was? Would I even want to tell her? What could I possibly tell her? Nothing had ever happened in my life worth telling except for meeting her. I was having feelings that I never experienced before. As crotchety as she could be I couldn't help but like her and I also felt bad for her; I wanted to take her in my arms and kiss her and tell her it would all be all right. If she would only look at life without such pessimism maybe she could move forward and make it what she wanted it to be and actually feel happy? It was almost as if she was stuck, unable to rid herself of all the anger.

After my first class I made my way. Every telephone booth I passed, I thought of calling her with some excuse as to why I couldn't make it. I'd been standing since ten-thirty holding a bunch of red carnations looking at the button with the tag next to it that read, 'Roche'. At 11 AM precisely, I rang her buzzer. She buzzed me in, and I walked up the three flights to her apartment. Her door was slightly open, and I could hear her talking to someone. I knocked lightly, and the door opened a bit more. Then Sarah swung the door open all the way, holding a phone with a very long extension. She put the phone down and signaled me to come in but not talk. I handed her the carnations, she looked at them for a millisecond miming an awww and then dropped them unceremoniously on a small table by the front door.

"The secretary? Really? How very predictable! Of course, I'm not surprised. You shouldn't be either, you should have known." Then she paused for a moment, winked at me and continued, "Has he found out about the tennis instructor?" She covered her mouth like a little girl having spilled the goods. "Mom! Please! I've always known. Mom! Stop yelling at me." Sarah said with a smug, revengeful look on her face, "I need to go now; I have to run to class. But I promise to call you back, bye! I'm hanging up now, mom, you do the same." She put down the receiver and placed the phone in the middle of the floor. "Hi!" she barked at me, sounding a bit manic, "How are you?"

"Good," I said. "Everything okay? Do you want me to come back another time? What's going on?" Sarah had an expression on her face that wasn't anger exactly, it was more like how the mad scientist looks in a bad horror movie moments before revealing his monster.

"Comeuppance, my handsome boy—comeuppance and karma, a bitch of a combination!" She said as she let go of a harsh, loud laugh. She sat on the couch and patted the cushion next to her, signaling me to sit. We had never been alone before, we'd always been surrounded by passersby, drunks and addicts—this was nice. "Sorry about the mess," Sarah said, not sounding particularly concerned. "My cleaning lady has been out sick."

I had never known anyone who had a cleaning lady. I was seriously impressed. I scanned the large room. From the look of things, her cleaning lady must have been laid up for quite a while. It was havoc. I'd never seen anything like it. Everything at my house was covered in plastic, and my mom cleaned it daily—seeing this would have sent her screaming down the street.

I stood up, thinking I would help straighten things out. I walked around the room realizing I didn't know what I could really do. Brown paper bags spilling over with garbage and take-out containers sat under the sink and just outside the cabinet doors, dishes with dried food particles—vegetarian, I assumed—except for what looked like chicken bones, sat piled precariously high in the sink begging to be washed. The bathroom sink, which must have originally been white, was now sporting spotty gray patches, and the mirror above the vanity was covered with dried toothpaste splatters and to finish things off, I surmised that the musty smell was due to the sitting water in the bathtub which obviously couldn't drain because of the clumps of hair blocking it.

Sarah lit sage and incense. The snakelike smoke curled around the room steadfastly attempting to cover up the myriad of smells in the tiny studio apartment. Even in my absolute, crystal-clear naiveté, I understood she was spinning her web. I sat down in the corner of her small sofa and looked at her. I giggled as I looked around for something to count—I always counted things around me when I got nervous, a habit I formed at thirteen the first time I masturbated, purely by accident I should say. In that case, I had to forget that my mother was in the next room and I was positive what I was doing was a mortal sin so I counted the tiles in the bathroom. Six hundred and forty pink and a hundred and seventy-two black bullheads. Now I wasn't sure what to count, maybe the dirty dishes in the sink?

Perhaps, I should take the lead. But I had no idea how to take the lead. She must have sensed my inadequacies. She offered me tea; I only drank tea when I had a cold. I reluctantly accepted, and she quickly produced a large vessel, a kind of ceramic amphora with two different-sized handles that seemed to have been made in a junior high school ceramic class, on the side of it her initials, S.C. "I love making art," she said proudly. She stood by the stove waiting for kettle to whistle. She was preoccupied with something. I could almost see her wheels spinning, I felt like I was intruding but didn't move or say anything. The whistle finally cut the deadly silence in and then I heard Sarah murmur under her breath. "It's about time!"

As I tried to negotiate drinking the tea without scalding myself, she walked over to the record player and picked up an album—on the cover a sexy Carly Simon is sitting on a wooden chair in an empty room wearing a silk negligee, one spaghetti strap hangs loosely off her shoulder as she sensually unfurls a translucent stocking over her leg. "Music always relaxes me." Sarah said caressing the cover. I attempted a smile. She took the record from the sleeve, put it on the player, and moved the arm into the third grove, dropping it on "You Belong to Me."

The tender piano strains oozed from the speakers. Sarah drifted around the room, singing, "Tell her, tell her..." but with an operatic quality—gaudy and lacking subtlety—as much as she tried, she would never have the sultry sound Carly possessed. "Isn't she perfect? She really knows what it's all about," she said, swaying like a willow branch on a windy day.

"For sure, for sure," I responded, taking another sip from the gigantic mug filled with piping hot, bitter tea. What did Sarah make this from? I wondered. Could it be poisonous? It was so harsh I could hardly swallow it. Sarah caught me wincing.

She said, "A little honey is nice," pointing to the little plastic bear with the yellow cap on the kitchen counter. "It's all natural," she cooed.

I smiled and let a very little amount of honey drip in my tea. She seemed so happy offering the natural honey in the little plastic teddy bear, that I didn't have the heart to tell her that honey made me gag. Since music was the topic of conversation, I figured I'd mention that I liked the Bee Gees and disco, at which point, Sarah almost had a meltdown.

"That's not music! It's commercial junk! Mindless, repetitive, gimmicky crap! It says nothing of what life's really about." I sank deeper into the corner of the sofa, holding my giant jug.

"Yeah, you're right, for sure. I just meant, like a long time ago, I liked them, but not so much now," I blabbered, unsure of what she was talking about. I didn't want to ruin the moment, but it was obvious I had. I wasn't sure what was in store for me and what she would do next, but I knew I'd upset her. "I really like the tea," I said as I lifted the vase above my head as if asking for forgiveness.

"You do know about what's really important, right?" she asked, her eyes wide and unblinking fixed on mine.

I was afraid to answer. I didn't know what was right and what was wrong, and as my head bobbed up and down and sideways like one of those tiny toy dogs on the dashboard of cars, I asked as I began to dislodge myself from the corner of the couch, "May I have some more honey?" She nodded, eerily reminding me of my father. Instead of going for the plastic teddy bear, I reached out and touched her hand. She then placed her other hand on my face.

"I'm sorry, I am passionate about what I know to be true," she said. And then she kissed me on the lips, just like that, like I belonged to her. It was so easy. Her anger melted.

Whoever said that ignorance is bliss had never been in my position. I had no idea what to do next. Except for my daily activity in the shower, I had no other experience to offer. I wasn't sure I should be participating in this—should I tell her? I was a virgin—a twenty-year old who had never dated a girl. I had never kissed anyone except my mom on the cheek. Sarah kept opening her mouth and sticking her tongue between my teeth. I tried not to let her tongue in, but then realized that's what was supposed to happen so I finally let her do it and thought that it may be a good idea to do the same to her.

I was so involved with figuring out the kissing I didn't realize what was happening next. She had her hand over my pants and was rubbing in the general area where my penis was, which was quickly responding, absolutely unconcerned with my total lack of experience. Fear, guilt and total ignorance. How could I go wrong? I had to do something. I closed my eyes and imagined myself showering, since that's where all my sexual experiences had taken place. I touched her breast. No bra! That was good. I wouldn't have known how to remove it had she been wearing one. I could feel Sarah breathing in my ear. She whispered, "Touch me."

I didn't know what else I should be touching since I now had both my hands on her breasts. "I am," I responded hesitantly.

"You're silly," she said in a very sweet voice, one I had never heard before. "I want you to touch me here." She guided my hand inside her baggy men's pants. She wasn't wearing underwear either! That I found strange. Suddenly I heard Brooke Shields in my head saying, "Nothing comes between me and my Calvins." This is what she meant!

As soon as my hand neared the area, Sarah moaned. It felt furry, puffy, and warm. And then, she whispered in my ear, "I love a man who knows how to perform cunnilingus." I wasn't sure if she saw the panic in my eyes. I didn't know the word. I repeated it in my head. Cunnilingus.... lingus.... tongue? Lick? Yeah, closer to lick. Taking Latin had come in handy after all. But the first part of the word...? By then, Sarah was gently pushing my head down, her sweater rolled above her breasts, so I started licking. She kept pushing my head further down until my face reached her belly. She stopped pushing. Instead, she ran her fingers through my hair as she gently pulled it—a sign that I should go back up? I thought. But I decided to stay put waiting for the next set of instructions. I had reached her bellybutton. I guessed that I had reached my destination so I started licking faster much like a child licking an ice cream cone. Sarah, giggled and said, "that tickles! You really are so silly!" She unzipped her man pants and holding my head with both hands much like someone getting ready to serve a volleyball, placed my face on a patch of hair. It all came together very quickly as to what the first part of the word meant. I didn't know that so much could happen in such a short time. Rainy Saturday mornings flashed in my head. That's when my father called my mom upstairs while she was busy making tomato sauce for midday dinner. He'd call and she would roll her eyes, go upstairs, lock their bedroom and twenty minutes later she'd come down, her face flushed, and return to her cooking. My parents could never do this, I thought. I wasn't sure I could do it.

I looked up and said, "I need to go to the bathroom."

"I understand," she said, which, of course made me wonder, why she would.

The smell of incense, burning sage, unwashed clothes, dirty dishes, garbage and Sarah's natural scents had suddenly made me nauseous. I looked around the bathroom and saw my reflection in the cloudy mirror. My face was beet red. But I couldn't chicken out. I looked around and spotted a box of Kleenex. I took one, ripped it in half and stuck it way up in my nostrils. I looked in the mirror and figured that the only way

Sarah could tell I had stuffed my nostrils was if she was below me. I walked out of the bathroom head down and, without saying a word, got on my knees, parted her legs and descended back into her dark forest. Then I caught sight of something, a twinkle of light just below my chin. There, among the thick curls of hair, lay my cross hanging from the chain around my neck. For a moment I truly believed my heart had stopped beating and all I could see in this patch of hair was my mother holding the rosary, Christ on a cross above her, and Father Termine and the nuns behind him swaying back and forth like the Pips behind Gladys Knight.

Sarah began wiggling her hips—I couldn't stop now. I closed my eyes and willed them all to leave. I grabbed the cross and swung it around my neck and inside my shirt. I let Sarah guide me. Her breath quickened, and she started moaning, and then she clasped my head between her thighs so tightly I didn't know whether she was enjoying what I was doing or she having a stroke. Her back arched like a bow and her moaning became deeper and quicker. With my ears cloaked between her thighs, she sounded like a faraway foghorn. Her body began to sway back and forth faster and faster, I heard calling out, but couldn't make out what it was she said and suddenly she let out a scream that seemed to last forever before her body totally collapsed like a ragdoll, seeming, for a terrifying moment, lifeless. I pulled back and noticed the two balls of Kleenex sitting there in the patch of thick hair, looking at me like a coyote's eyes hiding in a bush in the darkness of the night. Should I pick them up? I thought. Would she notice? But before I could decide, Sarah pulled me up and kissed me again. Her face was glistening with perspiration, and her cheeks were a deep red and seemed to almost be pulsating.

"I'm going to take care of you now," she said as she pushed me back on the couch.

I sat back as she easily unzipped my jeans. Like a surgeon preparing for that first cut, she reached inside and pulled it out. My head reeled just like it had years before in the shower. No one had ever touched me there except for me. Right hand, left hand or a combination of both, but this sensation was beyond anything I had ever imagined. I wondered for a second how Sarah knew how to do what she was doing. I held my breath and closed my eyes. I felt an intense pleasure. My heart raced and I tried not to yell as my body disappeared somewhere beyond this world, to a place of power and strength, where all that mattered was to reach the highest peak! The thousand voices that constantly whispered over and over again in my head that I was bad, that I was made of sin and should be punished were suddenly quiet. It was the most perfect moment. It didn't take long at all. Much like a jack-in-the-box, it popped out a little too quickly with a stupid look on its face. My bliss was over, way too fast. Sarah's eyes widened and her eyebrows arched as if she had walked into a room full of people screaming, "Surprise!"

"It's okay, it happens, you are really excited," she said as she reached for her scarf, wiping her hand on it. I blushed and looked away. I got up, and without making eye contact made my way back to the bathroom. I wasn't surprised when

I looked at the soap dish—no soap. I wet my hand and rubbed the dried crusted remainders of old soap bars in the dish until suds emerged. I quickly cleaned, washed, and rinsed. I stupidly thought I would find a clean towel. I reached for the Kleenex box again, pulled out a bunch and patted myself dry. Then stood there trying to pull off tiny pieces of Kleenex stuck all over my privates. It was a losing battle, I gave up, zippered up and then rinsed my mouth, all the while wondering how this was going to play out in confession that coming Sunday, I didn't have the words to share this with Father Termine, I would probably be struck down once I left Sarah's building, anyway.

I heard the phone ring. It rang and rang and rang—and for a brief moment I thought Sarah had left. But once the phone went silent, I heard her dragging it across the floor and then I heard dialing.

I walked out of the bathroom. The look of absolute disgust told me that she was talking to her mother again. She sat there on the tiny couch, naked, drawing circles around her nipples with her fingers. She blew me a kiss and gestured that she would call me later. I was going to wave back but then stopped. Instead, I stood there looking at Sarah, but she no longer saw me. I thought we would at least talk after what we had just finished doing. I waited, still looking at her, needing for her to turn toward me again and say something, I didn't expect I love you, but maybe an I like you? The incense had by now burnt out, all that remained were ashes. I looked around the studio for the first time. It was uncared for, used, but not appreciated for what it provided. I looked at Sarah again and she was completely oblivious to the fact that I was standing there. She was so taken by what she was being told by her mother whose crying I could hear clear across the room, that she still hadn't a clue that I was standing there staring at her. Sarah was biting her nails and pulling on her cuticles. She looked like an animal hovering over its prey about to strike one final time, finishing it off. It was then that I understood that it was she who had set the entire thing in motion. It wasn't enough that her parents were unhappy with themselves and their marriage, Sarah had to make them suffer because she had suffered. She had found a way to let each of her parents know what the other was doing. She had manipulated them into their pain.

The sound of her voice suddenly rang in my ears Alessandro! That's what she had yelled out moments before.

I reached in my pocket and pulled out my smokes. I lit one and stood there letting the smoke fill the tiny apartment, Sarah still oblivious to my presence. But then she suddenly spun around, eyes wide open, "What the are you doing?" she yelled.

"Watching and learning," I said dropping the cigarette and putting it out on the floor, "Watching and learning," I repeated as I picked up the carnations on the table. "Goodbye, Sarah." For the first time, she had nothing to say.

I stood outside the building taking a very deep breath and then letting it out. All the weight, all the fear, all the uncertainty was gone. Sarah was right about one thing; I was strong and determined and I would not allow anyone to change that. I wondered for a moment what my father would think of Sarah and what she would make of him. I wasn't absolutely sure, but something told me that they would probably hit it off. She might even make him smile.

Moonglade

"Twenty-six years together and you never farted in front of me. Don't you find that strange?" The words shot out of my mouth—I had not meant to say them.

"Is that why we are breaking up, because of my good manners?" My husband said while going through drawers pulling things out, holding them up unsure of what belonged to whom. He was packing, everything it seemed—quickly, momentum was key, I guess.

"It's not just about manners—it's gotta mean something," I said, trying to find the answer to a question one rarely asks.

Our framed wedding picture which usually sat on the right side of the dresser was now faced down. The bedroom filled with suitcases.

"You're losing your mind," my husband said, "you can see that right?"

He would never trust me again—ever, he said.

He'd overheard a silly conversation I had on the phone with my sister about our friend—a straight friend. That's when everything changed. After I hung up, he attacked me. "I heard what you said. You mean that you've always had the hots for him? The same guy that comes to our house at least three times a week, drinks our wine and eats our food? His wife and kids were here for the holidays, for chrissakes! Isn't he straight? One-hundred percent according to him; I guess he wasn't so sure after all. I'm going to ruin your lives!"

I tried to explain that it was all nonsense. He had nothing to do with it. A one-way fantasy I created. I felt really foolish, standing there, my arms rounded, fists planted on each side of my body looking like an overaged (and somewhat overweight) Superman on his way to retiring. My husband stood tall and firm, shoulders slightly back, nodding his head as he flounced out on his way to find yet another suitcase.

"Don't you see how absurd you are being? Nothing happened, ever!" I explained astonished, how could he be jealous over something so silly and what did he mean he was going to ruin our lives?

"It was the sound of your voice, something did happen— or you had it in your head that it was going to happen and it would have because you are like a dog with a bone, you never let it go until you get what you want. It wasn't infatuation. It was clear how you felt—I know you."

I looked at my reflection in the mirror across the room.

Did he know me?

The night we met I was eyeing a tall burly guy at the bar. I was sucking the last of my drink through a tiny straw, fantasizing what I could do with this man—I wanted him to come home with me. Instead, another guy walked up to me, holding two drinks. He seemed shy, the glasses trembled in his hands.

"I heard you order scotch and soda, right?"

I thought he was cute in a bookish, clean-cut sort of way, but not my type. I didn't want to hurt his feelings so I took the drink and smiled.

"Thanks, I was just about to order another."

The burly guy on the other side of the bar was making his way out with another guy who could have been his twin. It was weird. My fantasy bubble burst. It was the same disappointment you feel when waking up from an erotic dream just as you are about to reach orgasm. I had such an amazing night in store—in my mind. I faced the nerdy boy whose eyes were now intently fixed on mine, silently insisting that I not scan the bar for anyone else. I obliged.

The race was on.

It wasn't until the day we moved in together that the thought crossed my mind—this isn't love, is it? Is it supposed to feel sweet? Warm? Comfortable? Like putting an old sweater on a snowy day? Where were the fireworks? I hadn't heard any.

And before I knew it, there were the holidays and the families gathering. The looks of joy and relief that we had found each other. "They make such a beautiful couple—such decent guys." "Bet you they'll make great dads." Everything planned and on course.

Until one day you are leaning on the door frame of your bedroom, half in and half out, afraid of entering because your husband is furious and is spinning around like a tornado tossing clothes he doesn't want over his shoulders while neatly folding what he is taking.

He picked up a sweater and tilted his head, scanning it. He looked baffled, like he didn't recognize it.

"I like the color, must be mine," he said, tossing it in the suitcase. I didn't say anything. It was my sweater, he knew. I had worn it to dinner one night and asked him if he liked it. I remember him sizing it up and then taking another bite of his steak and saying, "That color...a bit young for you, don't you think?" I never wore it again.

That's where we were in our relationship, a jab here and a jab there. Out of the most mundane comment an argument could erupt. The only way I found to stop the inevitable was simply to not respond.

You begin to compromise when the person sitting across the dinner table looks vaguely familiar, like someone sitting across from you on a train, you've seen him before but you can't quite recall where and you are unsure if you should say hello.

Then one night, as he is packing his suitcases to leave you, you gaze toward the bay window and notice that there is a full moon. It looks disappointed. And you feel like you've failed.

That moon. That damn moon.

He had rented an old lighthouse on the Hudson River, now a B&B, that's where he'd planned to make an honest man of me. Was it late September or early October? It always angers my husband that I can never recall the exact date. But I do remember that it was a Saturday night, the air was crisp and the moon low and full. We sat on the dock, legs dangling trying not to spill the bottle of champagne or drop the two flutes we had found in the broom closet, of all places. We sat there silently, captivated by the rhythmic waves rippling toward us.

"Picture perfect," he said,

"What?"

He took my hand, "The moonglades."

I didn't know what moonglades were.

"Will you marry me?" he said taking my hand.

Silence.

We hadn't known each other very long—or known many other men for that matter. I should have said something like, can you give me a little time to think about it? We should explore more, it's all happening so fast! But I could see his hands trembling again and he had that look in his eyes, and I am convinced that had I said anything except yes, he would have jumped into the mighty Hudson. And then what? I couldn't go after him, I never learned to swim. So, timidly I said, yes. Then with a bit more gusto added, I WILL MARRY YOU!

He kissed me and holding my face with both hands said, "We should buy a house together. Why keep paying rent when that money can go to something that will be ours?" Real estate was the best investment. We agreed.

Debauchery was what I had in mind that weekend. Instead, it ended with a marriage proposal, a list of must-haves for our soon-to-be-purchased four-bedroom love nest and learning the meaning of moonglades: the bright reflection of moonlight on a body of water.

❋

Our life was a large puzzle, we thought all the pieces were there but we could never find that last piece to make it whole. Still, we always did the right thing by each other. We took care of one another even when we argued to the point of uncontrollable rage. One night, after I threw a bowl of salad against the kitchen wall because my husband found it "too dressed" the shit hit the fan.

"I hate you!" I yelled.

"Don't say something you are going to regret tomorrow." he responded.

"I just said I hate you! Isn't that enough?"

Frustrated I left the room and went to sleep in our guest bedroom/office/television room/library. (Our must-have four bedrooms had quickly turned to two when we realized what prices were like in Manhattan.) In the morning I heard him getting ready and sent a text,

Give me five minutes

I will drive you.

No response but I knew he'd wait. He had an endoscopy scheduled and they would not allow him to leave on his own because of the anesthesia. "It's all the crap you eat at night that gives you heartburn. You need to take care of yourself," I said as he got out of the car. "I'll wait until they call me to come and get you. Good luck."

"Thanks for driving me," he said without looking back.

"Of course, we made a promise, always there for you and you always there for me."

He stopped, turned around, avoiding my eyes, he said, "We should talk…"

"We should, just go. We can talk later."

But we never did talk. It was just another deposit in the piggy bank now chock-full of I hate you(s) – I've had enough(s) and you don't love me anymore(s)…

I should have said no to that first drink. I should have hurt his feelings and gone with the burly guy that night. How can one drink change your life?

Now I could never have that burly guy. Too late. I'm not what I was twenty years ago. My self-confidence gone, along with my hair and six-pack. I wouldn't resent any of it if only we had passion. If we were meant to be together forever then unapologetic, relentless passion should exist—forever. Making love is boring. Down and dirty sex is what makes everyone wake up smiling, feeling invincible.

Rekindling that wild side was our intention every romantic holiday we took. We knew it must still be somewhere inside of us. But instead of ripping each other's clothes off and swinging from chandeliers we usually ended up gawking at younger men wanting them more than we wanted each other. The wild side was still there just not for one another.

And now here I stand still leaning on the door frame of our bedroom looking at the "love of my life" who has never farted in front of me packing suitcases because I have a silly crush.

Where do we go from here? How do you dissect and separate the lives of two people who were joined together for better or worse? Who owns what? Why should I get fifty percent of everything when it was him who brought in more money? And what of the things we both love? How do we decide who the leather reading chair and ottoman we searched for two years and finally found in a tiny antique shop in Reading Pennsylvania goes to? We jumped around like schoolgirls when we spotted it in the window display. That's the chair we placed in the corner of the "library" so we could read the Sunday New York Times. But that never happened. We stopped getting the paper, and instead, scanned the articles on our phones, usually in separate rooms. Who reads the paper anymore, anyway?

And who still says I love you? I haven't heard those words in years. When was the last time either of us said them? Sometimes late at night, after too many vodka martinis, I roll over to his side of the bed and whisper the words in his ear hoping he is asleep because I'm afraid that the sound of them no longer rings true.

We did it for the right reasons, it was what was expected. The right reasons. What were those reasons? I can't recall and I don't think he can either—could it be we wanted to prove something to our families? To ourselves?

My crush on a man that I can never have and who would never have me is not the reason my husband is leaving me. It was time. We may have thought love came on a perfect night in autumn watching the moon make magic on the river, for some it may have, for us it wasn't time. Maybe if I had had a one-nighter with the burly guy, and his twin had asked my husband home, then things may have turned out differently.

Maybe we would have met again, much later, me and my husband, in another bar. A little worn, a bit dented, somewhat used and definitely more cynical, then maybe we could have fallen in love properly. And then maybe, with all that under our belts, he would have happily farted in front of me.

It Was Only Sex, After All

"We've talked about this," my husband said sternly. He was right. We had talked and talked, argued, agreed, disagreed and then came to an understanding: it was only sex, and we were adults. We were going to do this thing that so many of our friends seemed to be enjoying without any reservation or concern. It had been too long for both of us and neither was getting any younger—as evident in how long it took us to get out of bed in the morning. Sex had become a thing that others did while we gradually accepted the real possibility that we may never have it again. But it wasn't as if we didn't try— well, almost tried. At times, perhaps, at some dinner party, we looked at each other across the room and for a moment saw the young man we had met long ago. But those two young men were now receiving mail from AARP. When we tried to reenact moments from our past it usually ended with one of us pulling away, softly placing a nostalgic kiss on silent lips while a disheartened "I'm sorry" was whispered in the darkness of the room.

So, the decision had been made, rules had been set and agreed upon, well... kind of agreed upon. Nowadays, there is an app for anything you want, or think you want. This one was specifically of young men offering their services in exchange for a fee. So many of them. It was like shopping on Amazon. Everything was there: price, size charts, features, similar products, and, of course reviews. I could not get over how perfect they all looked. It was daunting, especially for someone who has always believed that only something flawed can be perfect. I told my husband there was no way I could step into a room with someone who spends most of the day in a gym and tanning salon. My body issues refused to even consider the idea. Hell, even their body hair seemed coiffed. The entire process seemed sordid, and worse, unlike Amazon, there was no return policy. We would not be engaging a model.

Instead, we signed on to an app that catered to meetings of the kind we were looking for. I was convinced that no one would be interested in us, thus releasing me from the anxiety that was slowly building since the agreement had been made between me and my husband. But I was wrong. Who knew that older men were the "in" thing for so many considerably younger ones? We were inundated with requests to meet. At our age, we had become a commodity. My anxiety spiked to new heights.

We finally chose someone, or rather, the choice was made for us because I ran out of excuses as to why the men who were offering themselves would not match up to our sensibilities.

It was going to be fun. Really it was. And the David and all of Florence could wait. It wasn't going anywhere. We had planned this trip for years, but somehow had never gotten around to it. Our jobs in the clothing industry constantly took us overseas on short and exhausting jaunts so when it came to vacationing, we usually booked relaxing cruises around the Caribbean. But now that we had the means and more time at our disposal, we finally decided to "see the world." Italy had always been first on our list—it was where we had most visited during our business trips, but had never had the chance to really discover it. However, our Italian vacation itinerary had now changed. We just didn't know how much.

"You done?" my husband asked impatiently behind the bathroom door.

"Yes, you can go in," I said. I paused by the door. "What should I wear?"

"You're kidding, right?" he responded almost slamming the door in my face.

I stood there for a moment and then threw on jeans and a black t-shirt, my go-to whenever I wanted to look hip. I ran to the kitchen, washed cups from our morning coffee, rinsed dishes, put everything in the cupboards, and wiped the counters. Then I decided to fluff up the throw pillows on the couch. The bed was made. I decided to unmake it. Then stepping back, I looked at it and decided to make it up again. The stranger would soon be here. What time? *Soon*. I looked at my watch. Why was my heart pounding so loudly? It frightened me. The tiny purple flowers on the peeling wallpaper spun around the room. Too much light. It needed to be dark and sultry and mysterious. I struggled to close the old wooden shutters; they simply would not stay shut; they kept swinging open. I pulled and held and tried to make them still. It was an old building, hundreds of years old. Then, with a slam, they held closed except for one shutter tilted to the left. It swung open halfway and would not budge. I should leave it that way, I thought. Looks like that's the right amount of light anyway. The sunshine was now replaced by a semi-dark gray light. The wallpaper no longer buzzed with flowers instead it pulsated with tiny black dots.

Music? Should I put something on? What? Maybe the loud thumping of my heart would be drowned out?

"I am going to get beer, or wine." I said loudly, standing behind the bathroom door. "Do you think that's a good idea?"

"Whatever you want," my husband responded. "Just don't take forever."

Soon, I thought. "Yes, I'll hurry."

The heavy wooden door shut behind me. I stood for a moment looking to the right of Via della Colonna and then to the left. I heard the buzzing of Vespas, a perpetual sound of the city. The buildings lining the street seemed to be protecting its occupants standing side by side, tightly shut, silent, concealing behind its massive centuries-old wooden doors, colorful landscaped courtyards and elegant homes with large open windows and billowing white curtains. The brown and gray colors of the buildings met the shiny cobblestones in a drab blur, and for a moment I felt as if I could not breathe, I looked up wanting to make sure that the blue sky was above, guiding me. The sidewalk was ridiculously narrow, so I stepped out onto the cobblestone street, making sure not to be run down by a gaggle of speeding Vespas that I was positive were just around the corner.

Where had I seen that convenience store? I decided to go left, —left was good, — I was almost positive that's where the store was. The vicoli were all so similar that getting lost was now the norm, at least for tourists like myself, regardless of paper maps or Google directions. Yet, no one seemed to care. People wondered, staring up, spinning like tops, mouths agape slowly being swallowed by the beauty of Florence—this city that had been made so very long ago by men and monsters. The decaying murals of madonnas holding babies, saints holding crosses, and crosses holding christs seemed to be everywhere. I was captivated and terrified of them all at the same time since they were now transforming into reproachful faces warning me of the consequences of the sins that were soon to be committed.

I struggled to put together the right number of coins to pay the smiling clerk who obviously was very happy that I had purchased four bottles of wine and twelve beers of various brands. It may have been easier to hand over a fifty euro note but that would have meant more coins in my pocket. I didn't have my glasses and couldn't distinguish the value of the coins so I stuck my hand out, filled with them, and allowed the now slightly annoyed clerk to help himself. He did, I trusted.

The thin plastic bags had been tripled to hold the weight of the bottles. Why had I bought so much booze? Perhaps in the back of my mind, I intended on getting the stranger so inebriated he'd be unable to perform? I breathed a sigh of relief when I was able to navigate back to Via della Colonna. My heart had quieted down but the fear in my belly remained. My cell phone dinged in my pocket. I gingerly placed the bags on the ground.

What's the exact address? the message read.

Via della Colonna 20, I texted, my fingers trembling as they hit the letters.

Cinque minuti.

I walked slowly. I didn't want to be waiting when he arrived. As I approached the building there was no one in sight. I guessed that five minutes in Florence is different than five minutes in New York. I would wait after all. I fumbled with my phone, trying not to drop it as I looked for the code to punch in on the pad. The three bags of wine and beer I was holding rattled. I figured it might be better to just place the bags down so as not to drop them while I was searching for the code. It was at that moment I noticed a tall, handsome, young man in running gear approach me. Damn! He is wearing sunglasses—not fair. I needed to see his eyes. Would they register any fear or apprehension as mine surely did?

"Ciao," he said as if he'd known me for years. He couldn't have been more than twenty-five, perfectly fit, his dirty blonde hair still wet from showering, it seemed. He had a trimmed beard and the whitest, most perfect teeth I'd ever seen. He smiled and for a moment I thought he would start laughing. What could he possibly have seen in us that he chose to meet us? We weren't repulsive by any means, but our bodies screamed of countless gourmet dinners paired with too many bottles of fine wine. If we moved the wrong way, our backs might very well give out or very possibly trigger our sciatica. It seemed to me that as couples grew old together, they slowly took on each other's ailments. Memberships to gyms were something we paid monthly, but we had seen the inside of them only on the day of signing up, when we pledged to visit at least three times a week. Why was this man here? I just stood there holding my phone and pointing to it. He must have thought I was an imbecile. He didn't introduce himself and so, neither did I.

"Do you need help?" he said in English. I was taken aback for a second,

"Just looking for the code to get into the building."

He took off his glasses but I quickly gazed down. I didn't want to see his eyes now; I just wanted to get this over with. After four attempts, I finally got the right combination and we were in the cold, dark lobby of the building. He clicked the light switch, and the light illuminated the hallway and the staircase at the end. The switches automatically turned off after a few minutes, so one couldn't dillydally or make small talk so I hurried down the hallway. It was not until I began climbing the stairs that I realized how heavy the shopping bags had become. I was determined not to ask for help. I fought to climb the five flights of stairs to our Airbnb. The stranger behind me had ample opportunity to stab me and rob me of my wine and beer. I didn't care. Anything to lessen the cramping in my hands. I was wheezing by the time I reached the front door of the apartment. Completely out of breath, I opened the apartment door and sprung in with the last bit of strength I had, flinging the bags across the dining table, their weight having now become that of large boulders. I could hear my husband in the shower.

"Husband is still getting ready. Wanna beer?" I said, trying to hide my inability to take normal breaths. He sat across the table from me as I laid out different brands of beer. "I didn't know what you'd like, or what this beer is like, not sure the wine is any good, maybe I should have gone to another store. But I didn't want to be late, well not that I would have been, I'm never late, it's just I don't know the city and might have gotten turned around and probably lost so…" Thankfully he interrupted me. I knew I sounded like a babbling idiot.

"I like this one," he said taking the bottle and twisting the cap off. "Would you like to share some of it?"

"No, thank you. I will have some white wine."

Share. The word hung in the air.

My husband walked in with a shit-eating grin on his face and with a confidence I hadn't seen in years. Somehow, he had dried himself off and dressed within a couple of minutes of us coming through the front door. He was wearing black slacks, a black shirt buttoned to the neck and a white handkerchief tied around his neck. He looked like an Italian fascist in 1939. *Why?* I thought, *why?*

"Hey! How's it going?" he asked the stranger, sounding practiced and a bit too loud.

"Hey, good, good…You?" the stranger responded, downing the remainder of the beer, his manner relaxed. It was almost disconcerting.

"Good, good, good! Glad you speak English," my husband said, relieved as if he had asked the stranger for directions to a restaurant. "Beautiful city you have here," he continued, picking up a bottle of beer and guzzling as if parched from having just run a marathon in a desert. Then he just stood there, swaying a bit, his self-confidence now seeming to deflate. Perhaps he was finally registering the reality of the scenario and what we were about to do.

No one said anything. It was only a few seconds, but it felt like an eternity. I looked toward the room. The tiny dots swirled, my head spun a bit and I took a deep breath.

"Okay then," I said, "since everyone is fine and somewhat hydrated, should we get on with it?"

I was closest to the stranger; I took his hand and pulled slightly. He sprung up and followed me into the room. My husband picked up the glass with the remainder of my wine and downed that.

We stood by the bed. I undressed as if I was getting ready for a yearly physical. I placed my clothes neatly on a nearby chair. When I turned the stranger was completely nude on the bed and my husband, having somehow undressed as quickly as Clark Kent turning into Superman, stood above him.

The stranger's body was exquisite, something I thought I'd be voicing about the David right about now. It was tight and covered with a perfect tan—clearly, he sunbathed in the nude. He wasn't overly muscular but everything was in proportion. He was smooth with just the right amount of hair, not too much, not too little. I walked toward him and my husband—my body suddenly felt detached from its surroundings. A hand reached out to take my hand, like lovers about to walk along a beach. Courage seeped in—vino veritas, I thought. The pas de trois began, awkwardly, without commitment, without clear direction, oblivious to what the outcome would ultimately be.

In the darkness of the room arms and legs entwined, adjusted, tensed, went back and forth trembling with pleasure and shame. Familiar scents combined with new ones, I held back, then felt myself being pulled in, deliciously teased, and I wondered whether I should try to give in fully, allow myself to let go, without fear, without a care in the world. I opened my eyes. The dots on the wallpaper were now tiny eyes dancing around winking, tearing but also smiling. A familiar kiss—my own eyes getting moist. It was a kiss from the past. It felt so good, so secure, but so far away. A foot hit the back of my head. I stood outside myself looking from above laughing at the absurdity of it all.

A sudden murmur in my ear. A kiss, a sweet passionate kiss. I opened my eyes and for the first time, looked into this stranger's eyes. They were beautiful, youthful and without any judgement. I wondered if my eyes revealed my anger toward him. How dare you be here? How can you take from me this man whose strength has given me the confidence and security I have needed in order to breathe? Why are you able to give him what he will no longer accept from me? You, a total stranger? He reached for him. I turned away, hating myself for doing it, but unable to accept.

The stranger held my head with both of his hands and

kissed me once again with such passion it frightened me. This was not what this was supposed to be. I turned to my husband, who seemed to be spinning in a spiral that was moving faster and faster away from me until I could no longer touch his hand or see his face and all I was left with were questions. When is love no longer enough? *It's only sex.* The words rang in my ears. It had to be or else everything I believed in all my life had all been a farce. *It's only sex.* It had to be. I looked at my husband again, his face now lighter, smiling, and for a moment, I could see the young man I had fallen in love with so many years before. *It was only sex.*

With the same directness as I had mustered in the beginning, I directed it to end, at least for the stranger. His breath grew deeper, faster, and more demanding until he reached his moment of ecstasy. Then I realized I was with him all along, every moment, until the end—his and mine. I had to get out. The stranger's hand still holding mine, I pulled away without looking at him and disappeared in the bathroom. My heart once again pounding in my chest but no longer from fear.

The water from the shower came out hot, as hot as it could be, burning my skin yet unable to wash away this profound sense of wretchedness. The question now was obvious—where do we go from here? Would this become a normal part of our lives?

I looked in the mirror as I dried myself off. I stepped back. Something about my face. It also seemed lighter, clearer, without shame, and then I saw the young man, the young man I used to be so many years ago, the young man whose heart would always believe in love. I smiled.

I went back into the bedroom. My husband and the stranger were getting out of bed.

"He made me come!" my husband announced as if he'd just won the lottery.

"Mazol Tov!" I replied. "Now that it's done, remember we have dinner plans."

On cue, the stranger left to shower.

"That was fun! Did you enjoy it?" my husband asked, hopeful that I had.

"Yes, it was nice. Strange but nice."

My husband came near me and took me in his arms and pulled me close to him. He held me closer than he had in a long time. Then he kissed me with the same passion he had kissed me on a warm night twenty-five years before. "I love you—you know that. I always will, no matter what," he said.

"Yes, I know," I said, taking his hands. "It was only sex, after all."

Joel's Promises

Naive; having or show a lack of experience, judgment, or information; credulous.

Hunched over his laptop, Michael read the Dictionary. com meaning of the word over and over again. He scans his desk—or rather, the farm table that serves as his desk—to make sure everything is in its place. It's something he does when he feels uneasy and needs to resolve a problem. Michael has always had issues with desk drawers. They collect all the things that one wonders whether to keep or toss; for Michael, it's most often the latter. He doesn't procrastinate; he just throws everything in recycling bins. He likes order on his table: one laptop, one notebook, pencils, pens, one purple *Cymbidium* orchid plant, and a few framed photographs of his family and his husband, Charlie. Everything in its place, no surprises, no loose ends, move forward and don't get distracted, same rules he applied to his career as a CPA. Principles he has lived by all his life, but recently his blinders were removed, and now he is lost, unable to make sense of the emotions that are overwhelming his very being, unable to process the obsessive thoughts that are persistently bombarding his brain and making his life a disorganized, incomprehensible mess.

He pauses at Charlie's photograph. "You lied, Charlie—something you said you'd never do!" Michael says out loud. "You weren't supposed to go first!" He picks up the frame and puts it close to his chest but then abruptly places the photograph face down on the table, not wanting to deal with these emotions right now. He needs to put something else in order. Again, he looks at the screen of his laptop.

Anyone can be naive, Michael thinks. It's not a bad thing. It can be endearing, charming even. He reads the meaning again, pauses, then thinks, who am I kidding? Maybe it's charming for a teenager; for an old man, naivete is kind of pathetic. He stands up, stretches his back. He lets out a yelp. Jesus, it's getting worse, even with physical therapy three times a week. Maybe I should take a walk, stretch my legs. He looks out the window. The street is lined with cherry trees, the lawns are perfectly manicured, no brown patches, and the pavement is immaculate. Michael likes the order of the neighborhood, except there are no people walking about, no one to say hello to or have a chat with. The streets don't feel real; they feel like a disturbing nightmare, houses made of cardboard ready to fly away, like the houses on the tour that he and Charlie took of the backlots of Warner Brothers Studio. The houses are sad, sitting there, waiting for someone to bring life back to their empty corridors and large empty rooms.

Both he and Charlie had their reservations about moving to Staten Island. They loved where they lived in downtown Brooklyn. They could walk anywhere or take a short subway ride and have anything they wanted: theatre, movies, art galleries, museums. Sure, the city was noisy and not very clean, but it was vibrant, and it kept the mind and body buzzing. But they were offered millions for their house. They didn't want to move, but Staten Island wasn't that far from the city, and they reasoned that they could still do the things they enjoyed. Since retirement was around the corner, why not make the move and buy a place there to be near family and split time between New York and their favorite idyllic Caribbean island, Turks and Caicos? Unfortunately, they never took into consideration the unpredictability of life.

He gazes down at the screen. *Lack of experience.* He reads that part over again. Then everyone is naïve to a certain degree. No one can have experienced everything in life. He looks at the two middle fingers of his left hand, they are bent and gnarled. Damn arthritis, there's gotta be something to fix this! Old age sucks.

He looks at his cell phone sitting next to his laptop. I miss him, Michael thinks—not like he misses Charlie, that's an anguish that feels so hopeless you think you are going to suffocate. No, this is something else, something he thought he would never feel again. That smile, Michael thinks, I miss that most of all. Michael then touches his lips—he can still feel the gentle kisses.

The worst part was not being able to speak to anyone about it. Michael wasn't sure how they would react. He felt a kind of pride, but he was also embarrassed. He was proud to have been wanted by someone half his age, but ashamed for having been tossed aside without rhyme or reason—or maybe not? There must be a reason, I have to know, he keeps thinking over and over like the scratching of a needle on a broken record. How can I have misjudged him? He promised. "I'm not an idiot," he says out loud. He is taken aback by the sound of his own voice.

Michael picks up his cell phone and taps WhatsApp. His message sits there, silent, two checkmarks. He received it, he thinks. They are gray, not blue; he hasn't read it. He pulls up Google. *Can someone read your message on WhatsApp without the checkmarks showing blue?* The answer is there before he can blink. *WhatsApp offers a privacy option to let users read chat texts without letting the sender know.* He looks at the name on the top of the app. *Joel, last seen 9:39 AM.* He must have read the message. Why isn't he answering?

"It's creepy as shit," his cousin, Sam, states adamantly as he ties a white apron around his waist. He punches each word as he signals his assistant chef to cut the pieces of a pineapple smaller. Sam is fifteen years younger than Michael but has a good head on his shoulders, and Michael has always respected his opinion and has often taken his advice. Sam is taller than his older cousin but carries a lot more weight and looks several years his senior, probably due to the long days and nights spent working in restaurants most of his life.

"It wasn't James who looked for this guy. He reached out to him." Michael says trying to sound nonchalant about the story he is sharing with the one person he can talk to about anything in the world—except this. He might have gone to Miriam, his sister, but she would see right through him. It's all happening to Michael's friend, James; Sam would buy that. It's better that way, he thinks. Michael isn't ready to be judged or fixed or reprimanded. He wants an ear. Michael wasn't sure how his cousin would react to him showing up at his restaurant out of the blue while Sam and his staff were still prepping for the night's dinner, but once he came up with the James story, he called an Uber and went straight there, hoping he would not lose his courage and change his mind midway.

"It doesn't matter. A thirty-year-old doesn't go after a six-ty-four-year-old man because he falls in love. C'mon!" Sam enunciates slowly as he begins filleting a large tuna. "He wants something."

Michael stares in wonderment as his cousin begins the operation of scraping the scales off the tuna. Michael wraps his scarf tighter around his neck, wondering how everyone else is wearing t-shirts and not shivering from the cold air blowing in from the open back door of the kitchen. "Like what?" Michael asks, pretending not to know exactly what his cousin is about to say.

"Money? I don't know, his car? Taking control of him and then manipulating him to the point that he walks away with everything he's got?"

Michael winces as Sam begins scraping the guts out of the fish. His stomach flips as blood flies from the fish and onto Sam's hairy arms. The head of the fish, having been detached from the body, now sits to the side, its dead eyes staring up at

Michael. He steadies himself against the table, afraid that he might actually faint. He isn't usually so squeamish, but lately nothing about him is quite right.

"No! It's not like that," Michael pauses, knowing his voice sounds angry. "This young man has a very good job, has a nice place," he continues, "and James wasn't born yesterday."

Silence. They both break into laughter.

"Look, I'm not judging James or his young stud. Maybe it just has to do with kinky stuff. Maybe this kid has a fucked-up need to be with an old man… I don't know. It just doesn't seem right to me," Sam says as he finally tosses the gutted fish in a bucket of water and begins washing his hands.

"No, it doesn't," Michael says almost to himself.

"James fell for him. Didn't he?"

"Yeah, he did. Hard." Michael avoids looking at his cousin's eyes, not knowing whether he is shivering from the cold or from the words just spoken to him.

"I'm sorry. Tell James, I'm sorry he is hurting."

1982

Michael is sitting in a rust-colored Plymouth Satellite Sebring on the corner of Christopher and West Streets in Manhattan. He worked all through high school to save money to buy a car—it wasn't easy—school during the day, evenings bagging groceries, bussing dishes at the diner on weekends, and tutoring neighborhood kids in math. None of the jobs paid enough, but Michael was patient and eventually had just enough to buy a used car he named Betsy. He's just turned twenty-one, and he feels like an accomplished man, except for the secret he has kept to himself all his life. Week after week, he has been driving to this corner, parking, sitting, watching, never leaving his car.

It's a balmy Saturday night in early summer. The windows are shut tight except for the driver's side. It's down a few inches. Michael can hear the distant thumping coming from inside of Badlands. He can make out the song—it's his favorite. His body begins swaying as he imagines himself jumping on the dance floor. Outside of the bar is a dam of men wearing tight Levi's jeans, some wearing t-shirts, some not, many sporting full-leather outfits complete with peaked-leather caps adorned with chains. Michael watches. His heart races as his sweaty hand holds the handle of the car door. He badly wants to open the door and walk toward this crowd of men who seem so comfortable in their own skin, touching one another, laughing while several embrace tightly, heads buried in muscular hairy chests, but Michael is scared. He lights a cigarette and lowers the window a little more. He inhales deeply, and as he exhales, he rounds his lips as small circles of smoke glide out. Smoking usually calms him, but not in this moment. He flicks the cigarette out.

He wishes he had someone to talk to. He's read about this pneumonia gay men are dying from. "It's what they deserve," he'd heard a man on the subway tell a woman next to him. "They wanna be animals? So, that's what they get." No one seems to care, Michael thought.

The door of the bar opens, the music gets louder, two men come out of the bar, dragging a third. They just make it to the gutter when the man begins vomiting. Michael looks at the headline of the *Village Voice* lying next to him in the passenger seat, "Mysterious Disease Killing Gay Men." He wants so much to be free of this weight he has been carrying, but even as he's thinking this, his hand moves from the handle of the door. He takes the steering wheel while the other feels for the key in the ignition. The engine suddenly roars, the car idles, begins to slowly roll as Michael looks in the rearview mirror, the crowd becomes a blur like his own existence. This is the point in his life when Michael retreats, a decision that through the years made him wonder if it was cowardice and not fear that made him run, leaving everyone else to deal with the loss of so many and not having had the courage to stand for himself and for those who would suffer and die.

September 2023

Dear Joel, I am writing this note because I've not heard anything from you in weeks. I texted you several times on WhatsApp as you asked me to do but haven't gotten any reply back. I thought that perhaps something was wrong with my phone? Or yours? Or the app? And I didn't want you to think that I was avoiding you so I decided to go old school and write this card. I don't trust the post office, so I decided to drop it off along with this small gift. I know how much you like to go to the gym so I thought you might make use of these work-out gloves. Do let me know you got them. I will wait for a text. It would be okay for you to call me though, if you wanted to. I hope you do. I think of you often. A big hug, Michael.

Present Day

Michael sits by the window. The rain hasn't stopped for days. He despises the rain but is also comforted by the rhythmic sound it makes. He stands and picks up the cell phone yet again, checking for messages, texts, anything. Silence. He looks around. He has just vacuumed, polished the furniture, mopped the floors, organized his books, shredded papers, everything in its place and looking spiffy. He looks at the photographs on the baby grand piano. Why is this thing still here? he thinks. Charlie was the virtuoso. I can't play. All it's good for is to showcase photographs and collect dust. Michael has been avoiding looking at certain photos, the ones with Charlie, his husband, the man he thought was going to take care of him until he passed away, but who instead died before him. Michael cannot forgive him for that. He is angry and has no idea what to do with that anger, and worst of all he hasn't been able to cry.

1993

"Hello? Hi, Miriam? It's me. Yeah, well, of course. Who else would it be?" Michael's hand trembles as he holds the receiver of the telephone. He is sitting on a bumped-out seat of a bay window in a midnight-blue Victorian home, looking out at Alamo Square Park in San Francisco. Charlie sits across from him, silent, smiling, proud as a parent watching his child receive a diploma. "I don't know when I'm coming home just yet. You see, I found this job here, and the weather is nice… I know it was supposed to be a temporary job, but when an opportunity…" Michael's voice trails off.

"Hello? Are you sure that's all you want to tell me?" Miriam says slowly, staccato like, as if talking to someone who speaks another language. Michael pictures her cubicle at work in one of those nondescript glass skyscrapers along Madison Avenue. He can sense she is looking at the overflowing photographs thumb-tacked on her cork board: baby pictures, wedding parties, graduation photos all there to put on a smile in her heart in those moments when the cubicle closes in on her and all she wants to do is run for her life. He knows his sister like he knows his own heart.

"I've met someone… I'm not sure how to say this."

"Just say it," Miriam responds impatiently. "What's his name?" She pulls off a photograph of her and Michael sitting around a large round table at some wedding. Smiling husbands, wives, fiancées sit with their heads leaning on one another. Michael had no plus one, so he had asked her. It had become the norm, Michael and Miriam, Miriam and Michael, side-by-side at all family gatherings and all of his friends' weddings.

"What? How?" Michael says loudly, springing from his seat.

"That's it right? It's a man. That's what you wanted to tell me. Michael, I've known for a long time. I've never said anything because I thought you didn't want me or the family to know. You are thirty-two years old. It's time you found someone. Before it's too late." She catches her own reflection on the dark computer screen, a reflection of a woman resigned to be the big sister, her parents' caretaker, everyone's favorite spinster aunt. Would her life have been any different if she had not always been there for Michael? For everyone that needed her?

"I've never done anything, Miriam. I've always played by the rules..." Michael injects, sounding desperate.

"I know that! So go, enjoy yourself. Stay away if you need to, for now, but come back, right? Come back? We all need you to come back," Miriam says, her voice cracking as she puts down the receiver. Michael knows she is crying; he knows she wishes with all her heart that he'll find the happiness hoping that through him she could maybe feel the joy her own heart so desperately yearns for.

After ten years in San Francisco, Michael and Charlie move back east to be near their families and Miriam.

March 2023

Michael is looking at the screen of his iPhone. The little mailbox icon has a red dot—a message—that's what the app's guide explained. Michael looks at it. He scans the living room as if expecting someone to be there ready to reprimand him for being a foolish old man, but he can't deny the anticipation bubbling in his belly, excited that someone has contacted him. Foolish or not, he taps on the mailbox icon and a message pops-up.

"Hey Daddy, how's it going?"

Michael stares at the screen unable to move.

"Nice fur. Wanna chat? Joel here." A second message reads.

Michael looks at the screen and locates the member's profile. The photograph is that of a young man. He taps again and other photographs slide by—the young man in a bathing suit, his body perfectly chiseled and beaming a warm friendly smile. Other photographs show him catching a baseball mid-air, in another his arms are up, looking exhausted but exhilarated as he crosses the finish line of some marathon he'd just run. He can't be more than twenty-five, Michael thinks, though he says he's thirty. He reads his profile. *I am into Daddies, dating, and having fun. Ask me anything. No face pic no response!*

Michael had decided not to put a photo of his face. He wanted to be anonymous—he wasn't sure why. Was he embarrassed? Perhaps, or was it just the remnants of a past lived in hiding and excuses? He didn't expect to do anything, but he was curious to see what it was all about, so not showing his face was also a way of being a voyeur without fully committing to the reasons he was there. Sex? Well maybe, maybe yes, but more than that, he thought it might be a nice way to make friends. So, he posted a few photos of his chest, his best feature he felt, one in a suit with his face hidden, and one of a close-up of the lower part of his face, showing his gray stubble—they should see that I'm not a spring chicken, he had thought.

Michael finally decides to respond to the jubilant young man who seems from his photographs committed to savor life without care or hesitation, something Michael has longed for all his life. "*Do you realize how old I am?*" Michael asks, certain that the response would come back with a quick and apologetic, oh sorry, I didn't realize. Instead, Michael's back straightens, tilting his head, as he reads the response to his question.

"*Yeah, that's what I like. Older men are hot.*"

April 2020

Charlie is lying in a hospital bed in the middle of the living room. Michael runs in and out of the room unsure of what he should be doing. His niece, Sidney, a nurse at NewYork-Presbyterian who works in the emergency room, had warned, "Don't bring Uncle Charlie to any hospital. They won't let you see him. They don't really know what to do. Some patients don't even make it through the night. Keep him home, I'll help you." So, their living room became a makeshift mini-hospital, complete with an oxygen tank, a vital sign monitor, and every and any medication being recommended by doctors—which seemed to change on a daily basis. No one was really sure of anything. It was just the beginning of the pandemic.

It had been almost two weeks with no change, and it was

obvious Charlie was getting worse. His oxygen levels kept dropping, and even the oxygen didn't seem to be working. A life-long smoker, Charlie had only quit a few years before when a lung screening scan confirmed emphysema. The inhalers had kept him going, but now this virus had made it almost impossible for him to take breaths.

"Stop," Charlie says almost inaudibly.

"I don't know what to do. Was this a mistake? Maybe we should go to a hospital, maybe they can do more." Michael is now frantic; the beeping of the monitor is driving him to insanity, and he is terrified that he will lose the only man who ever truly loved him. Nothing makes sense.

"Just wait, sit and wait with me," Charlie says, struggling to make his voice loud enough to be heard.

Michael carefully lays next to Charlie, placing his head near his shoulder. He is about to remove the N-95 mask that his niece was able to get a hold of after calling in every favor possible, but Charlie stops him.

Michael begins to cry. "I want to give you more time. I want us to live it all over. It's not enough time, goddamn it. It was only yesterday we met. I won't let you... Maybe, maybe..." Michael looks up at Charlie. He is smiling.

"Shut up... near me." Charlie's voice isn't there. It's been replaced by raspy wheezes. Each word is agony, and joy. "We... had a great life. You can't make everything right... I'm sorry, to make you sad. I've loved you so much."

"I know, stop talking, save your energy. Sidney is bringing a doctor friend later, if they can make it out of the hospital.

You'll see, we'll find a way out; we always do. I love you so much. You were the only man in my life and the only man I ever needed." He takes Charlie's hand. It's cold, almost stiff. He tries to warm it.

Later that night as Michael waits for a miracle, the beeping of the monitor suddenly slows. Michael doesn't move. Each slowing beep feels like a blow to his gut. It beeps again, then trudges to the next beep, crawling slowly until the final beep turns into a steady, solid black line that wraps around Michael's throat making it impossible for him to scream.

March 2023

Michael responds, *"I'm not sure about this, can I have a minute to think about it?"*

He stares, waiting for the red dot on the mailbox. The seconds seem like hours. Did I lose my chance? he thinks. Should I just say yes and not show up if I change my mind?

"You have thirty seconds," responds Joel, followed by a smiley face and a question mark.

"Oh, okay..." Michael types and presses send before even finishing his sentence.

"Kidding," Joel quickly types back. *"Take your time, I want you to be sure."*

What do I say? What do I do? I wish Charlie was here. I could ask him anything, maybe not this—definitely not this. Michael looks over the piano and at a photograph of him and

Charlie at a Halloween party dressed as Bill and Hillary Clinton. No one knew who we were, Michael laughs, but we loved thinking we were the most powerful couple in the country.

"Charlie," Michael says out loud, "Do you think I should meet a man who was in diapers when we met? He thinks I'm the best thing since sliced bread." Michael closes his eyes and puts his hands together as if praying. I'm sure that this would go over well with Charlie. Would he tell me to take a chance, as he often did? Michael picks up his phone and types, "*I will meet you, but just to introduce myself and see if I am who you really want. Is that okay?*"

"*Great! Name place and time. I'll be there,*" Joel quickly types back.

"*You can pick the place,*" Michael types and then hurriedly adds, "*But if either of us doesn't feel like staying, then we must be honest and tell the other.*"

"*My word, I promise to be honest, I will.*"

The next day Michael is parked in front of Alchemy, a neighborhood bar he'd never been to but has driven by many times on his way home. I wonder what kind of bar it is. He lowers his window and tries to hear whether there is music coming from the bar. Nothing. It's fifteen minutes past the meeting time. If I don't do this, I will never forgive myself. He quickly gets out of the car, clicks the fob, and as he is approaching the door to the bar, he hears someone calling him. "Michael?" It's Joel.

"I'm so sorry I'm late. I hope you were not leaving. The train took forever. I'm glad you are here." Joel is now holding the door open for Michael. He is taller than I thought he'd be, Michael thinks. Joel's excitement is so real, without any reservation. It's refreshing, contagious in a way.

They are sitting at one of the booths. Michael has figured out that this is just a bar. The crowd runs the gamut from straight to gay and everything in between. Neither he or Joel has said much except the usual: What will you have to drink? Would you like something to eat? This is a nice place. They exchange looks. Michael keeps thinking of whether he has trimmed his nose hairs or if the bright light above their table is casting shadows of his nose medusas on the table. Did he pluck those three gray hairs that insist on emerging from his ears every two weeks? The doubts persist, but then his thoughts turn back to another time, to another bar when all he had to do to prepare was shower and dry his black curly hair, spray some cologne on his neck, and he was ready. He is reminded of the first time Charlie asked him out for drinks. Michael was so nervous he could hear every stupid word he spoke echoing in his ears, yet he couldn't stop talking until Charlie reached over the table and took his hand, and suddenly the world quieted down, and all he could hear were whispers in a perfect world, a world he had for so long hoped to live in without the constant fear that someone would find him out.

Holding his second artisanal beer with a name that Michael has never heard of, Joel finally asks, "How's your scotch? Can't drink that stuff myself, but I like a man who does."

"It's fine, smooth, thank you," Michael says, realizing that he is finishing his third drink, and the temperature of his body has become warmer, softer, more welcoming. "Perhaps I'm drinking too much?"

"No such thing," Joel interjects quickly. "You are so handsome. I thought you'd be hot, but you are really very hot."

Michael looks around the bar for a moment, unsure how to respond. Then after swallowing the last drop of scotch, he clumsily says, "You are so beautiful, your hair is so shiny, your eyes so blue. And your smile is intoxicating."

"*Intoxicating*! Wow! No one has ever said that to me. I want you." Joel reaches for Michael's hand across the table. Michael lets him take it and then suddenly pulls away, looking around the bar again.

"Can we go and talk in my car? I feel like everyone is looking at us and thinking the worst about me."

Joel stands up before Michael has a chance to finish his sentence. "Let's go, now." Joel hurries towards the door. "Not the car—my place. It's just a few blocks away."

Michael walks beside Joel, who is chattering about how great the neighborhood is and the deal he has on the rent of his apartment because his best friends own the building. Michael kind of registers the words but has nothing to say in return. When they arrive, Joel opens a side door to the building and proudly announces that he has his own private entrance. Michael hesitates for a moment but can't help but follow Joel's smile. He is now being invited to turn back the clock, to buy back time, to return to a place where life has no end, where every road is full of possibilities, where ignorance is bliss because youth is blind. The door closes behind him, and before either of them says another word, Michael reaches for Joel's face with both hands and looks deep in his eyes. A lighting of energy shoots through his body, and he kisses this young man, feeling time melting away until he too is young and strong and unaware that life is fleeting and death is just moments away.

Present Day

"I had a feeling you were James in the scenario. Did you think I would judge you? After everything we've been through," Sam says, sounding hurt. He pours another shot of single malt scotch in Michael's glass. They are sitting at a four-seater. The white tablecloth is marked with stains from red wine and spilled food. It's late, the restaurant's lights are dimmed, everyone has gone home, and a sense of finality drifts in the air.

"I'm sorry, Sam, I am so confused. I'm frustrated, I'm happy, I'm sad, I'm elated, I'm disappointed in myself, and I am so angry I could scream. How can I, a sixty-four-year-old man who has had a successful career, who had a once-in-a-life-time relationship with a man that came from heaven, who has friends and family that love him, feel so lost? I feel like I never grew up. I don't understand anything that I'm feeling."

"It's normal," Sam says, throwing the words away. "I'm sure it's happened to many, many people. We all want to be wanted, it's the most natural thing in the world. It makes us feel good."

"He made me invincible, Sam. Every time l was with him, I felt like I was a new man, strong and loved in ways I hadn't been, ever, not even by Charlie. Joel made me feel like I was the only man he could ever love. What I don't get is how someone could kiss another person, make love to them, and then just forget about them."

"It's called hooking up. That's all it is. People do it every day and then move on. Why can't you move on?" Sam's tone is no longer the tone of someone consoling, instead, it's stern and direct. "This is not about him; this is about you. How can you give him so much power over you? He's a punk! If he was a man, he'd say what's on his mind and then cut ties. Let it go, Michael. He has. Don't you understand that he doesn't feel for you what you feel for him?"

For the first time in the conversation, Michael doesn't have an answer. Sam reaches over to hug him. Michael turns away, like a child who has been reprimanded by his kindergarten teacher and now is being patted on the head for crying.

"I'm sorry," Sam continues, "the last thing I want to do is hurt you. But unless you break ties with this guy, all you are going to feel is pain. Do you really want that in your life? Isn't it time for you to enjoy all that you have worked so hard for all these years?"

Michael again doesn't reply. How can he explain that after Charlie's death he feels like he's been falling into the abyss and that just the smell of this man makes him feel young again? Joel's skin is new and not shrinking, it's alive, tight, sweet, and nowhere near death. And how can he explain that he feels like he's won a prize of a million years of youth? Michael knows it's not his own, but it feels like it is, and he needs it like he needs the air to breathe so he can go on hoping that life has not abandoned him. Michael has never experienced what he feels for Joel, and that makes him wonder whether his entire relationship with Charlie was just based on an idea of love rather than what real love should feel like; love should be all-encompassing—but, then, he also questions. Is what he feels for this young man truly love? Or is it lust? Or is it his own inability to face the inevitable end to his own existence?

"I know I should cut him out of my life, Sam, but I don't know how to let go. I know I shouldn't feel like this at this stage of my life. I know I should have more control, but each time I decide not to think of him anymore, I feel like I'm dying a little, as if there is nothing left to look forward to. I know it sounds insane, but the wondering, the guessing, the hoping, even the waiting, keeps me alive."

March 2023

They are face to face, naked. Michael unable to look anywhere except in Joel's eyes. They kiss as Michael runs his fingers through Joel's thick youthful hair. The young man begins stroking Michael's chest. "I love your hairy chest." He then licks his thumb and forefinger clipping Michael's nipple. Michael closes his eyes. He is frozen for a moment but then he roughly pushes Joel on the bed. Joel laughs, "Woah! I knew it!" Michael lunges on top of Joel like a lion pinning down its prey. "Slow…slow…slow…" Joel murmurs taking his arms and wrapping them tightly around Michael. Michael softens. It's suddenly 1982 again but now he is getting out of his Plymouth and walking toward the men outside of the bar. They are all smiling at him, arms wide open. He walks up to them and they all embrace him. "Now," Joel demands. "Now."

December 2023

Hey Joel, just wanted to follow up. Believe it or not this is all new to me. I thought it a joke, a man your age wanting to meet a man my age who looks like me. I told you I didn't understand young wanting old. But I tried giving you what I thought you wanted. I was there when you needed me. There were so many things I wanted to do but, because I didn't know if I should or if it was in the playbook, I don't know if I did something wrong, if there is something you hate about me now, my body, my face or something I said that ultimately turned you off—but I'd like to know, I just want to understand. Joel, I like you… I thought I could know you. I trusted you, maybe I was wrong. Someone recently told me I am naïve. Perhaps, I am, but being naïve means not having experience too and even at my age I don't have it in this type of situation. As strange as it may sound, it's the truth. Joel, I like your smile, your kisses and thought if anything, we could be friends and see each other once in a while. You don't owe me anything, I know that, but can you help me understand? If you liked being with me even for a moment and you are willing to let me know, please tell me what it was about me that made you not want to see me or talk to me anymore. I know you didn't say it, but my gut says otherwise. A chat by phone, or a quick meet would mean so much.

Michael waits to press send and when he does, he holds his breath, wondering whether he has made a fool of himself yet again. He decides to go for a walk and leave his phone on his desk. He needs to feel in control at least for an hour. The next day there is a message.

Good morning, Michael, I promise to get back to you with a longer response in time. You didn't do anything wrong or anything to turn me off. You're a very sexy guy. Promise to get back to you soon.

Michael stares at the text and reads it over and over again. He then thanks Joel for responding and writes that he will wait to hear from him.

"Take your time Joel, I want you to be sure." He presses send. He stares at the phone with renewed hope and waits.

Martha's House

A floor-to-ceiling picture window gives way to a breath-taking view of the majestic Hudson River. Her eyes are fixed on the gray shadows undulating just beneath the waves. The river always mystifies her, her consciousness having become, at some point, without her realizing it, a part of its movement. The light, the colors, the soft sounds it makes dictates how she feels—constantly guiding her and she desperately needs to be guided by something that doesn't want anything in return except to be appreciated. But even the beauty of the river cannot make her life whole again.

She sits in the corner of the L-shaped sofa gently petting the tiny white long-haired Chihuahua sleeping on her lap. Poor little thing, she thinks. Miss Dubois has been abandoned too, in a way—they did not fight for her, they had no need for Miss Dubois. She found that disheartening. It felt almost vicious.

As the day becomes evening her expectations once again begin to dim. This time of day both hypnotizes and terrifies her. The barges sailing up and down the river carrying what look like piles of rocks, finally stop coming by. The weekenders have gone back to the marina with their jet skis, sailboats and mini yachts. She imagines them meandering in their gardens filled with flowers tended to by some local gardener. What will they do now? Have dinner? Dance? Perhaps, make love?

"Everyone has found their place, except us," she says as she continues softly caressing the tiny dog. She looks over at the closet leading to the mud room. Its door is ajar. She can see the wedding gifts piled one on top of the other. Their bows by now flattened, some corners crushed when she forced them into the small closet and a thick layer of dust has settled on them. It frustrates her that for some reason she's afraid to open them. She feels a paralyzing ineptitude she's never known before.

Will it be another uneventful Saturday? Does she have the courage tonight to make her move? A sudden gust of wind wafts through the room. She looks around and places her hand on Miss Dubois; strangely, she wants to make sure the little dog is still breathing. The temperature outside reads 72 but the room is very cold. She stacks several logs in the fireplace and lights the flame. The blue, orange, and yellow glows engulf the firebox and bounce around the hearth.

"Don't you think it's a bit off scale for the room?" she had asked her husband.

"Martha thought it should be the focal point of the room. She asked the builder to make it as big as possible, 'It should make everyone feel warm,' she would say."

It did warm up the room, but it also looked as if it could swallow you up, never to be found again.

"I see," she'd responded. She did not argue the point, there was no way around it. It was, after all Martha's house and even though she was gone, the sometimes-grandiose aesthetics the first lady of the house had decided upon were as immovable as the very foundation the house was built on.

It had been a year, just a year, and her life had become a surreal soap opera—even she smiles at that thought. Her husband dead, after three months of marriage. He had been a widower and she a divorcee. It wasn't a love affair to end all love affairs but it was nice, comforting, to have found each other especially after discovering that they'd grown up a few blocks apart in Flatbush, Brooklyn.

It happened so suddenly. She was in a showroom at a car dealership looking to buy a baby-blue Mustang convertible. He was there to lease one. It felt planned, she had thought, like a cut in a movie where characters are quickly transported to the near future without a past ever having been lived.

"It's a beauty," he'd said.

"I've always wanted one. But my ex-husband thought it wasn't a practical car to buy."

"Leasing is better, you can write it off as a business expense," he said as they both stuck their heads in to look at the interior.

"I don't have a business, and besides, leasing makes it feel like it's not really yours. Like you are borrowing it. I like to own it. I want it to belong to me." She said this a bit too forcefully, as if she was referring to something other than the car.

Then she added, "At this price it better belong to me!" She laughed. And so did he. After that, they were inseparable.

A few lunches, a few dinners, a few strolls in the park holding hands and an awkward, yet sweet night of love making and he proposed. She accepted.

"Do you love me?" he asked.

"I think so, do you?" she replied.

"I think so," he responded.

That seemed to be enough for both. They made it official on a cold December day as they strolled along the icy river. He slipped on her finger the prettiest vintage emerald engagement ring she'd ever seen. How truly beautiful, she had thought as she lifted her hand to the sky. How incredibly unique. Until one night she found a photograph of her husband and Martha in a small drawer of his nightstand and noticed that Martha wore the same exact ring. She looked closer at the photograph wondering why he would ever do that. But then she opened the drawer and placed the photo back. She wasn't disheartened or angry; instead, she thought, he must love me as much as he loved her. She was relieved.

She suggested that they both sell their homes and have a fresh start. He seemed hesitant at first, but when he saw how much it meant to her, he finally agreed. But he insisted they buy a home with a view of the water, the river, a lake, perhaps a beach house. She agreed. They both needed to look at something that was constantly moving. He seemed happy about that, but she could not let go of the nagging feeling that secretly he hoped she would change her mind and stay in the house he and Martha had built.

She worked diligently on the wedding registry, choosing

contemporary pieces that looked more like Ikea than Bergdorf Goodman. Martha's tastes felt to her a bit pretentious. Too many flower patterns, too much gilt, too much of everything. They seemed untouchable. She would never say that to him.

Their ceremony was held in the garden surrounded by their families and a few friends all looking on in their own skeptical way. She knew that they were wondering how they could have fallen in love so quickly, him so soon after Martha's death and her only nine months after her divorce. Had they known each other in a prior life or were they desperate not to be alone for the rest of their lives? Even she thought it strange. But there it was.

A romantic honeymoon to Hawaii was booked. Neither had been there. Her ex-husband had never cared for vacations that entailed long flights—he'd preferred long boring drives to neighboring states.

After the wedding she hoped that regret would not rear its ugly head for either of them. She so wished for fun and true happiness for both. But they never made it to their romantic honeymoon. He had this insistent pain in the abdomen that radiated to his lower back. He'd also started losing weight just before the wedding. Nerves, she had thought. But soon it was apparent something was wrong. He couldn't keep anything down. His coloring had changed. He brushed it off by saying that it was probably a stomach thing. She trusted him. After all, he'd been a general doctor before retiring. Still, she convinced him to go for tests. When he returned, his face could not hide what he'd been told. Pancreatic cancer.

In sickness and in health, she had thought, but shouldn't there have been an out clause? She felt petty and guilty for even thinking such a thing, but she had looked after both her sick parents, and she wasn't sure she had the strength to listen to the desperate groaning, to wipe him clean, to give false hope to dying eyes—she had been there for their final breaths and she didn't think she could go through all that again. "No! This can't be happening!" she yelled as she stood in the wind and rain watching the crashing waves of the river. They would fight it, seek the best care possible. It was not going to end this way.

She sat still, holding her breath as she watched him take his last one.

The will was read in a small stuffy conference office in New Haven, Connecticut. She and his three daughters sat around an oval conference table, their arms slightly brushing together. She gazed down, tracing the veins on the Formica table, unable to look at anyone's eyes. She felt uncomfortable.

The old attorney seemed to feel the same as he stood up and taking a step back announced that the will was recently amended. The daughters' backs straightened; they emitted soft growls like angry peacocks ready to attack. They looked quizzically at the attorney, no longer seeming sorrowful as they had attempted to portray when first taking their seats at the table.

"What do you mean, the will was amended?"

"After your mother's death your father instructed me to name his new wife the beneficiary of his entire estate." The attorney mumbled almost not wanting to be heard. His hands trembled as he held the will. He'd been warned by his client that his daughters would definitely spin out of control.

The three simultaneously jumped out of their seats. One of them screamed, "What did you do to our father!?"

Another shrilled, "He would never leave you everything! He barely knew you!"

The words hung, demanding an explanation.

"I took care of your father while he was dying," she said.

"I bet you did!" the youngest daughter yelled, spewing venom.

"You..." the eldest said pointing a finger toward the attorney as if holding a dagger, "you will hear from our lawyers!"

One by one they left, slamming the door harder than the previous one had.

"She'll be sorry..."

"Money hungry whore!"

"Conniving bitch."

Their exclamations faded slowly as they clomped down the hallway.

She finally looked up. The frazzled attorney reached for a glass of water, his hand still trembling.

She and the attorney traded observations. Her husband had pancreatic cancer, he had not been demented before dying, he knew what he was doing.

She understood the reason why he'd left everything to her including the house, all of Martha's paintings, and Miss Dubois, Martha's little dog. He once told her that he'd been lucky in love having found two wonderful women to be part of his life. But he hadn't been so lucky with his children, he had never really liked them as people. They were demanding spoiled little snots who took and took, demanding everything, expecting everything while never giving anything in return, not even love.

No one came to visit after that.

"Don't give the paintings away, please, don't let anyone take the dog! Other than that, you can do anything you want to the house," he'd said in moments of consciousness as she fed him pills from the box delivered by the hospice nurse with the prescient, knowing eyes.

"Mom, why did you sell your house and move up there?" her daughter asked the last time they spoke on the phone. She did not have a logical answer. She felt like she had to be there. Even though this was the house that Martha had designed and Martha was everywhere, she knew she had to be there.

"I don't know. I just know that this is the only place where I can sleep."

"How can you sleep in that house where they both died? I really don't understand it."

Neither does she at times. She often wonders if it is normal to only be able to rest in a house where so much sickness and pain took place.

"Do anything you want," she keeps hearing his voice saying. But she is unable to. Every time she makes a decision to change the color of a wall, or move the furniture around, she hears, "Martha was a designer at heart, a wonderful painter.

She studied art, loved the theatre, visited hundreds of museums all around the world, she was a true Renaissance woman." Even when she tends to the garden she hears his voice, "Martha was a master gardener. She planted those rose bushes. The height of the lilac needs to be lower—Martha pruned it so as not to block the view of the river when sitting on the Adirondack chairs." She often thinks, Martha was the perfect wife, I can't hold a candle to her so what did he see in me?

At night she tries to make sense of it, even though it says on paper that the house belongs to her, she can't change anything in it. Hell, she thinks, she can't even reorganize the kitchen cabinets because every time she tries, she hears, "Martha thought…" or "Martha felt…" or "Martha said…" And every night as she struggles, she inevitably falls into a profound sleep where dreams don't seem to exist.

"Goddamn it!' she yells, "Tonight, I am not going to simply give in to sleep." Determined, she walks toward the closet where her wedding gifts had been tossed in like second-hand items to be donated to charity. She takes the boxes with their flattened bows and places them on the dining table. The shiny silver wrapping paper looks dull. She tears small pieces of paper off of the boxes, letting them fly around her like confetti at a carnival. She holds a box with a card taped on it. The handwriting looks hurried as if written without care in a moving vehicle. "Congratulations on your wedding! May you have many happy years together, All the Best, Harris and Season." All the best, she thinks, from the heart, really! She drops the note on the floor, opens the box and takes out an asymmetrical bowl made of glass. She walks over to the sideboard stacked with Majolica-like bowls and plates, picks up one of the largest clay bowls and replaces it with the glass one. She frowns. She reaches for it but then steps back tilts her head and looks at it for a moment.

"Looks a bit out of place, doesn't it, Miss Dubois?" The tiny dog trots toward her, its collar jingling. She picks her up from the sofa. "Eventually, it will fit in—it will just take a little time, right?" Miss Dubois licks her on the neck; she receives the gesture as an approval. Her heart lightens. She returns to the couch and looks at the bowl. It's beautiful, she thinks. She strokes the tiny dog with purpose—she now belongs to her.

Suddenly, timed picture lights burst to life over all of Martha's paintings. For a moment she is startled, but then she smiles.

"Not all at once. Slowly, I promise," she whispers. "But it needs to be done." She settles more comfortably on the sofa. "It's time."

Wonder Bread

Federico sat, slowly eating his toast, savoring every bite as he swung his legs swiftly back and forth and looked around the kitchen. He got up and stood by the refrigerator. It was almost twice his size, he figured. The round white belly-shaped range didn't have a tank with propane like back in Genoa, like back home. Instead, the hose disappeared behind it and was attached to the wall. Sitting back down on the chair with the stiff plastic white and black cushion he gently wiped the cool Formica tabletop with the palm of his hand. Its chrome legs, once shiny, had begun to rust. He took another slice of bread.

It was the scent of Wonder Bread toasting that woke Federico that cold November morning in 1969, one day before his first Thanksgiving. He had eaten toasted bread with butter and jam in the old country, but that was harder, crunchier and it broke apart easily, making a mess with all its crumbs. Everything about this new bread was different. It made him happy. The flawless loaf neatly wrapped in its soft white plastic bag bursting with blue, red and yellow dots, sat on the table seeming to smile at him. The sight of the slices toasted just so, shining with melted golden butter embraced him. He felt protected. It was, if only for a moment, perfection.

Just yesterday, they had landed at the TWA terminal at JFK Airport. It had been the family's first time on a plane. Federico's ears felt as if they had been packed with cotton balls. He stood in the cavernous glass structure watching people rushing by. Along with his mother and sister, Claudia, they waited for his father to arrive. Claudia was thirteen—four years older than Federico. A pretty girl with long, shiny chestnut hair which she nervously twirled around her fingers. She stood next to her mother, looking around, whispering to her that they should make sure that all their suitcases had arrived, it was all they had and they couldn't afford to lose anything. Her deep brown eyes held a mature, defiant gaze—perhaps because their mother had so often confided her own stories of sorrow, making the young girl appear older before her time.

Sandro, their father, finally arrived, their grandfather steps behind him. Sandro walked toward Federico first. He seemed oblivious to his wife and daughter. Federico put his arms around his father's neck and kissed him on the cheek. He smelled of Old Spice cologne, his black leather jacket, and whiskey. "Ciao bello!"

Federico pulled back and ran to his mother's side.

Margherita stood silent, stroking her son's hair as he clung to her waist. She avoided her husband's eyes. Sandro slowly surveyed his wife. Margherita's deep dark brown hair was styled a la Brigitte Bardot. She wore a black turtleneck, black slacks, black patent leather high-heels and a black fitted coat that hugged her body and accentuated her movie star shape.

Sandro cleared his throat, walked closer to his wife and said, "Why are you wearing pants? Do you know what that means?"

She looked at him for a moment, then with an upturned eyebrow she replied with the sweetest voice she could muster, "Yes, it means I'm comfortable." Then she looked at her father-in-law. "Should we get the bags? The kids are tired and hungry."

The children's grandfather nodded and taking the hint, began to walk quickly toward the baggage claim. They all followed.

Claudia trailed him closely as he made his way down the long corridor. "Nonno," she called out, "we haven't seen you in so long. You always look the same."

He smiled, slowing his step to a more dignified stride. His head rose a bit higher than it had been. "Grazie, bella!" he said with delight. His shiny silver hair was combed back, every strand kept firmly in place by pomade. He wore a two-piece plaid beige suit, a crisp light blue shirt and a gold patterned tie. His camel hair overcoat was unbuttoned, collar up, as a silk yellow scarf dangled from his neck. The ever-present scent of talcum powder wafted behind him, lingering even when he was no longer there.

After some awkward hugs between Sandro and his daughter and guarded smiles between Sandro and Margherita they piled in a car that to Federico resembled a small boat with wheels. It was brown and he spelled out its name to his sister as their grandfather opened the trunk, "V-A-L-I-A-N-T."

"It's like a bus!" Federico exclaimed. "I never saw one in Genoa."

"Probably because the streets are so narrow, it wouldn't fit," Claudia said as she got in the backseat with her mother and brother.

Their grandfather said it would take them about thirty minutes to get home. Instead, it took over an hour, mostly because he couldn't find the airport exit and kept winding up in front of the TWA terminal. No one said a word, not even Sandro, who kept lighting one cigarette after another and whose face seemed to be turning purple. Grandfather kept blaming the confusing signs and cursing whoever had designed the airport. It seemed they would never get out until Claudia finally said, "Why don't you just follow one of the buses that say New York."

Sandro turned, looked at his daughter and winked. Claudia smiled tentatively at her father and then lowered her eyes. Without another word being spoken, their grandfather did just that—shortly thereafter they arrived in Brooklyn.

They got out of the car and looked up at the six-story prewar tenement building that was to be their home. It was identical to the rest of the buildings lining the street except that some were vacant and their windows had been smashed while some had been burned down by their owners for the insurance money. The streets were white from the salt spread by sanitation trucks in anticipation of the snow storm the city was expecting. The sun struggled to penetrate the slow-moving gray clouds. The frigid wind reached the bones, Margherita and the children shivered—they were not accustomed to this extreme cold.

Their grandfather's new wife, Teresa, known as Tessie, owned the building; she had not wanted the newly-arrived family there. Tessie was a woman whose suspicious eyes and pursed lips revealed a constant anger and perpetual mistrust, probably because she had never known how it felt to be loved. Tessie had a daughter by her first husband but he had abandoned Teresa shortly after the child's birth, saying in the note he left on the kitchen table that he just didn't like her and couldn't take being near her another minute.

Her current husband stayed solely for what Tessie could provide. He hoped to one day get his hands on her money and properties.

Tessie stood in the doorway of the apartment with a half-smile on her face while wiping her hands dry on a frayed dish towel she kept tucked on the side of her apron. She had given it her best shot to try to look happy to see them, but had just come across as insincere and forced. When Federico and Claudia went toward her to say hello, she moved back, allowing them in, but didn't hug them. She patted Margherita on the back and said, "This is your new home."

The apartment was a railroad flat. This one, however, had a bump-out on its left side that many would consider a walk-in closet. "You will sleep here," she said to Claudia as she pointed to the tiny area furnished with a small cot and a small wooden crate meant to be used as a nightstand.

Tessie walked toward the back of the apartment, and

everyone followed. They stood in the doorway of a dark room with a double bed and a rickety dresser sitting atop four bricks. "This is for you and your husband," Teresa said to Margherita, who had remained stone faced since entering the apartment.

Then walking back toward the living room, Tessie said to Federico, "And *you* will sleep over there!"

In the living room, he looked around, confused.

"Over there! It turns into a bed. It's almost new!" Teresa announced defiantly while pointing to a gray recliner tucked in the corner of the room. The chair clearly had been used as a scratching post by one or more cats.

"What do you say?" Margherita implored.

Claudia mumbled something, and Federico ran to his step-grandmother, put his arms around her waist, and said, "Thank you!"

"Ah, okay. He's sweet," Tessie said as she gently pushed him away. She patted him on the head and wiped her hand on the dishtowel.

She placed the other hand on their Margherita's shoulder and said, "It is what it is. What are you going to do? Your husband," she continued, "didn't lift a finger. He showed up yesterday. That *puttana* he keeps in Connecticut dropped him off."

Tessie paused, trying to gauge Margherita's reaction to this news, and then added, "Are you sure it was a good idea for you to come here?" She guided Margherita into the living room away from the children.

"I had no choice. He stopped sending money. There are

no jobs in Italy. How could I provide for them? I have to try. I'll talk to him and convince him. Maybe if we spend some time together with the kids…" she stopped and for the first time really looked around the room.

A television sat in the middle of the two front windows with shuttered blinds. The curtains looked as if they had been recycled from the train of an old-fashioned wedding dress. They had tiny embroidered flowers and were torn at the edges. They were stiff, as if starched way too many times.

Margherita sat down on a small sofa whose arms were worn down and whose cushions showed faded stains, and hid scents of past spills that now had been unsuccessfully camouflaged with Lysol. It sat strategically in the darker part of the room, seeming embarrassed by its imperfections.

A small brown coffee table—scratched, chipped, and painted with too many mismatched layers of brown finishes and waxed within an inch of its life—sat center stage. It held a stained, tattered doily with a Capodimonte basket with dozens of tiny colorful (chipped) ceramic flowers. Margherita's drawn face could no longer hide her inner turmoil.

"Hey, I did the best I could," Tessie said.

"Oh, I know, I know. Thank you. It's all very nice," Margherita responded meekly.

That night, she hoped to speak to her husband. But Sandro had left after dropping them off and didn't return until morning. Margherita fell asleep wondering if she had made the worst decision in her life leaving Italy for this.

※

The following day, they all gathered at Tessie's apartment across the hallway from theirs. Sandro sat at the oval-shaped kitchen table drinking wine. He smiled when he saw his son enter the apartment—but he didn't say anything. Claudia and Federico stood for a moment huddled by the door before taking a seat across from their father. Margherita joined Tessie in the kitchen to help prepare the holiday dinner.

Unlike the family's sparsely furnished apartment, every inch of this one was crowded with furniture and cardboard boxes stacked halfway to the ceiling. The living room resembled a stock room with tightly packed racks of clothing, dresses, coats, and nightgowns. In between the racks a loveseat had been placed where three men sat on its edge holding small recycled jars of Nutella filled with red wine while staring at a small television set that teetered precariously on a small folding table. The console of a bigger television hid behind a pile of stacked boxes. One of the men held a white handkerchief that he would now and then wipe his forehead with.

Grandfather replenished wine for guests, then gently pulled Federico by the shoulder and lead him outside the front door of the apartment.

"Come on, help your Nonno. We need a board to put on the table so everyone can sit," he said, draining the last of his wine.

They walked outside to the side of the building and took the stairs down to a walkway. At the end of the walkway, Federico could see the courtyard where piles of garbage sat. His grandfather grumbled, "They toss the garbage out of their kitchen windows, that's what happens when the garbage men go on strike, *animali*!"

They approached the basement door but stopped before it. It was ajar. "Never just walk in. First, bang on the door. Hard. Step-back and wait. If someone is inside, they will run out. It also helps if there's rats."

And then he did exactly that. He pounded angrily, stepped back, and regarded the door like a trap that might spring any second.

No one ran out and Federico hoped that if there had been rats, they would have scampered away. His grandfather then walked in slowly with his right arm extended. He pulled on a cord hanging from the ceiling and a single lightbulb lit up, barely giving any light to the darkness of the cold, wet, musty room. Federico could make out some walls jutting out; he was convinced that monsters were hiding behind them. He could feel the slime under his shoes. He didn't know whether to wrap his arms around his grandfather's body or run out.

He heard his grandfather cursing under his breath as he reached for a lighter to shed some additional light. Federico stepped carefully behind him as his grandfather reached what seemed to be the middle of the room. There on its side was the plywood. It was covered with indistinguishable bugs making their way around in circles, perhaps creating a permanent place to call home. His grandfather reached for an old rag hanging by a nail and cleared away what he could see. Then Federico helped him lift the board toward the safety of daylight. His grandfather grunted as he pulled while Federico's small hands struggled to keep hold of the corner of the board.

It was at this moment when Federico's eyes grew accustomed to the light. Against the wall, he noticed metal garbage pails, dented into disturbing shapes. As he walked by them, he could see the crusty bottoms. They buzzed with crawling insects feasting on the putrid remnants and on what seemed to be, each other.

He tried to turn away, but then he saw them, a man and a woman, hiding behind the pails. Both faces staring with dead, glassy eyes toward him. Their emaciated bodies twisted and tangled like children playing hide and seek, hoping to have become invisible. Beside them a dirty spoon, books of matches, and a rubber hose—a needle stood at attention, still stuck in the woman's arm.

Federico dropped the corner of the board and opened his mouth to scream but nothing came out. His grandfather turned to see his grandson's terrified face. He then finally noticed what the young boy could not take his eyes off of.

"Son-of-a-bitch!" his grandfather said, "Turn away, don't look at them and don't say anything when we get upstairs. I'll take care of them later."

In what seemed to Federico like slow motion, he and his grandfather finally made it outside. He had been holding his breath so long that he felt like he would faint, but instead he inhaled the cold air and filled his lungs until he couldn't inhale any more air, hoping to become a balloon so he could float toward the sky, toward any other place other than the hell he had just been to.

His grandfather winked at him as they set the plywood on the oval table. Sandro stood in the living room talking to the three men, who were now standing in a small circle looking uncomfortable in their ill-fitting suits. Now, Sandro was holding a tall glass of scotch slightly diluted with soda water.

Claudia helped set the table. Once done, Tessie yelled, "C'mon, sit down! It's almost ready over here!"

She stood by the stove, producing more and more food like an endless multicolored magic handkerchief being pulled out of a magician's sleeve. She wore a shabby, loose-fitting housedress but each of her fingers flaunted a ring with a different colored gem and around her neck were several gold chains. Off the lowest hanging chain there was a cross that sparkled with dozens of small diamonds that caught the light in every direction she moved.

Tessie liked to show off her gold and diamonds because she knew the power they held over her husband. She knew why he'd married her. Tessie met him while on holiday in Italy. He was a maître-d at a seaside restaurant in Naples. They were both widowed. She saw a handsome older man who could entertain her when she felt lonely and he saw a rich Italian-American woman with lots of diamonds who could make him very comfortable in his old age. But she held everything she had close to the chest, never giving him control of anything. He hadn't planned on that. As much as he resented her for it, he spent day after day professing his love. He also hadn't planned on being the superintendent of a tenement. He had envisioned a house in the suburbs. But Tessie wasn't going to sell and leave the biggest asset her father had left to her and not to her brothers—she wanted to prove she could manage it and make it profitable.

Tessie filled the plates and Margherita passed them around. Once everyone was served, the two women sat down.

"Buon appetito!" Tessie said loudly.

After the obligatory compliments on the abundance of the food and appreciation for all the hard work, silence fell over the long makeshift dining table as everyone began eating. Federico stared at the three boarders, their heads down except to nod once in a while, looking up toward Tessie and mumbling, "Buono, buono." They weren't family and they didn't behave like friends so Federico didn't understand why they were at the table. But later as they were cleaning up, he overheard a Teresa and his mother talking.

"I need to make ends meet," Teresa said. This was a lie, according to what Federico heard his grandfather tell Sandro earlier in the day as they shared their third glass of whiskey. According to his grandfather she had plenty of money and jewels—he'd shared this information sotto voce, making sure Teresa was nowhere in earshot. His grandfather said that telling everyone she was scraping by was her way to keep people from asking her for help.

"So, I got a few dollars in the bank!" she explained to his mom, "But, you do what you can and make some more. I rent rooms, feed these poor *disgraziati* and sell whatever the drug addicts steal from the downtown shops. Your father-in-law isn't working, he's useless, he is only good for one thing," and then she winked.

Federico saw his mom put her head down. She looked uncomfortable and didn't reply. She continued scraping the leftover on the plates into the garbage. "No, don't toss them in trash," Teresa ordered, making Margherita freeze in place. "Whatever scraps are left, toss them out the kitchen window. It helps the rats stay near and helps keep those drugged-up losers away. When they get desperate for a fix, they will break into any place to steal." His mom's head snapped up her wide eyes looked terrified.

Meanwhile, the men, still sitting at the table, oblivious to any chore that the women may have needed help with, continued picking on pastries as the wine flowed easily. They then began discussing soccer and the lack of games shown on American television. Federico and Claudia sat bewildered, staring at the huge turkey in the middle of the table, wondering if it was real. No one had wanted to eat it. After the platters of salami, prosciutto, and mortadella surrounded by different cheeses and bowls of olives; after the platters of stuffed mushrooms, red peppers and eggplant rollatini; after then baked ziti, pork ribs and sausages that simmered for three hours in the gravy used on the ziti, no one could even contemplate touching the turkey and fixings. "Fine," Teresa had said, standing up, both hands on the table looking menacing, "Whatever is left over, you will all eat all of it for lunch and dinner for the next week. Are we clear?" In unison they all nodded.

Federico stole glances at his father. He hadn't seen him in

years except for the rare trips he made back to Genoa. Claudia often repeated to Federico the stories she'd been told by Margherita, even details that perhaps should have not been shared by a mother to a young daughter. After they got married, their parents had agreed that he should keep working on ocean liners crossing from Genoa to New York because they paid the highest wages—the plan was to save up money to open a family restaurant in one of the beach towns along the Riviera. The voyages between the cities lasted two weeks, but it wasn't like it would be forever. Sandro had worked on ships since his teens—that's how he learned to cook. He had risen from third cook to chef in just a few years. It wasn't his passion, just a way to earn a living.

Years before he had a job lined up on the *Andrea Doria* but missed boarding it because he was at a card game, refusing to leave until he won his money back. When he heard that the ship sank after colliding with another ship, he felt his luck had been with him after all. But the sinking of the ship haunted him. Every night it was the same nightmare: surrounded by bobbing dead bodies, he was drowning. Boarding a ship became difficult so as time went by, he fortified himself with scotch and the courage to board. The nightmares came only while at sea. Sometimes when he docked in New York, he would miss the return voyage. Those times became more and more frequent and the weeks turned into months and the months into years. On his infrequent returns to Italy, he'd bring money, gifts and the same promise, "One more trip and when I come back, we will open that restaurant."

But that day never came. Margherita knew there was another woman—that is, after the many other women she had known about before. His shipmates regularly reported to her on their return. She'd call and they would offer up excuses for him, but then admit to the real reason why he had "missed" boarding the ship, again.

Margherita knew how easy it was for Sandro. A smile, a wink and a tilt of the head as he ran his fingers through his thick jet-black hair, and women simply gave in. They wanted to take care of him, to save him, to protect him as she had once wanted to—but his demons would not let go. Those demons were rooted in his soul from his youth and he could no longer control them except to try and escape them if only for a moment with sex, with alcohol, with the possible win of a horse race. And when those things failed him, he'd become a demon himself, threatening and violent. Margherita had experienced that violence and it was terrifying.

In the past, Federico heard his mother say that her husband loved "drinking, women and horses more than anything else in life." He wondered if this man had any love left for them. What was happening at this table, on this Thanksgiving Day, didn't feel much like love. This stranger had no idea who his children were. And yet, he was the reason they had come here, to reunite with him.

Later that night, Federico could hear the angered whispering of his parents coming from the "master bedroom." On hands and knees, he made his way down the dark hallway, crouching so low to the ground he almost disappeared into the cracks of the wood floor. The door was open and he hid in the corner just outside of the room, in the darkness. He wondered where Claudia was. Then he noticed her in the corner of the room. She was in a fetal position on the floor holding her head, covering her ears. She looked like a snail that had retracted so far into its shell that one wondered whether it had died within itself.

He couldn't see his parents except for their shadows on the wall. Sandro was swaying, trying not to give in to the effects of the whiskey and fall to the floor. He steadied himself by holding one hand on the headboard of the bed while the other rose above Margherita's head, in a fist ready to strike. Then suddenly Federico noticed his mother's shadow rise above his father's, transforming her body into an eagle, talons wide and ready to strike down her prey. Furiously, Margherita swiped down, mercilessly cutting deep into his flesh. Sandro recoiled, his hands now wrapped around his face.

"Go back to your whore," he heard his mother say. "I can take care of my kids on my own. You can't take them! I am not afraid of you anymore!"

"How?...You?" Sandro managed to say.

"It can't be anymore—it just wasn't meant to be," Margherita said, as if to herself.

Sandro and Margherita had been apart for too many years. Too many accusations of infidelities had been made and there had been too many moments of solitude where an embrace would have meant hope. All this had cemented their relationship and what had been true love at the beginning had slowly been ripped apart like vultures plucking at a dead carcass.

Before Federico could retreat to his recliner, his father staggered by him without noticing his only son trembling within his own shadow. Stunned and defeated, Sandro stumbled down the narrow hallway to the front door, never to be seen again, leaving his wife and children once more to wonder what their lives would become.

Federico went back to his recliner. He tried to sleep but he couldn't help thinking that now there would be no white picket fences, no bicycles on manicured lawns waiting to be ridden to a best friend's house. There would be no songs or laughter or anything that remotely looked like the America he had seen back home in those black and white shows, the America he had thought would be waiting for them when they arrived. He cried, silently, not wanting to be heard, flooded with deep disappointment in the Mouseketeers, who had shown him what life could be if he only believed. Well, he had believed, but none of it had come true. They had all lied, he thought, as he flipped and flopped atop the recliner, which was, he knew, not truly a bed.

Days later, Margherita sat the two of them down and announced that for the next few months they would need to buckle down until they could go home. She would open up a bank account, go to work and save enough money for them to return home. Federico and Claudia decided they would take the colorful drawing paper they had found in a kitchen drawer along with a box of crayons and make a calendar. Claudia used the edge of a magazine to make lines and turned those lines into weeks. Then she drew little red, blue, and yellow flowers on all the Sundays and used a different color to write the name of the month. They didn't know how many pieces of paper would make "a few months" so they decided to use six. They then made a hole on the upper right corner of each page and strung them together with a piece of orange yarn.

As the weeks passed, he and his sister were able to put another red X on the calendar, but something was happening. They saw less of Margherita. She was always at work until late at night to show the boss how many coats she had sewn to-gether. Then she would sit at the kitchen table counting "the tickets." She looked tired, older than her age. And each day Claudia became more like their mom—getting Federico ready for school, going food shopping and preparing whatever meal she had been taught to make so that Margherita could work just a little longer and bring home more tickets, which meant more money to deposit in the bank on Saturday mornings be-fore she went off to the factory to work a few more hours.

Night after night, Federico tried to escape as he lis-tened to the men's voices outside his windows. They yelled and threatened as they played games of dominoes that had begun as friendly challenges but soon turned dangerous af-ter beers had been consumed and insults about wives veiled as jokes began to burst out of the mouths of the losers. Many of these nights ended with sirens blaring and the police trying to figure out who had pulled out the first knife. And on his convertible recliner that turned into a bed, Federico waited, hoping to create an opening for sleep to creep in.

In this new world there was never a moment of silence. Federico missed how back home, in Genoa, after the midday meal everyone lowered their wooden blinds to make their apartments dark and cool. And for the next hour or so everything would stop. Cats furled on the hoods of parked cars, finding sleep in the warmth of the sunlight. Everything was silent except for the occasional mewling of a baby refusing to give in to sleep. This was his favorite time of the day. He'd pretend to close his eyes for a nap and as the others settled in their slumber he would sneak on the balcony and look out at the vastness of the city that seemed to sigh into a calm comfort knowing that its inhabitants were resting. He'd stand there looking hard toward the horizon where the sea blazed with sparkling sun glitter. He imagined a ship docking and on that ship his father would stand tall and mighty, waving both arms smiling toward him. He'd arrive home, bringing Federico a castle filled with knights, horses, a king, a queen and dozens of villagers. Federico would sit in his room and make up stories as he played, while his father wrapped his arms around his mother and sister as he vowed never to leave them again.

But in this city they had been brought to, people were constantly moving and buzzing around like bees swarming around a hive. The sounds of people yelling, fighting, children crying and music blaring never stopped. He felt trapped in this run-down building, in this neighborhood resembling a war-torn village, in this colorless city whose streets were littered in garbage stuck to cement sidewalks by the frozen ice. And no one seemed to ever rest.

Another six pieces of colorful paper were strung together with the orange yarn. Margherita needed more time. The bank book didn't have enough for them to return home. As much as she tried, she couldn't put more money away to make it happen, especially now that Tessie expected her to pay rent. The children couldn't show they were upset. They had to be strong and help Margherita count tickets and kiss her when she was down and hug her when she needed strength to go on.

At some point, one of the boarders began to drop by. He and Margherita would sit at the kitchen table and talk about Italy, his situation, her situation, their hopes. He always arrived bearing silly gifts, things he picked up from Woolworth's on Washington Avenue.

That year winter seemed to never end. By then, Federico had been placed in school but not Claudia. Tessie had made inquiries and according to the guidance counselor, it was too late for Claudia to enter school and it would be, according to their step-grandmother, "Better if she stayed home, with me, for the next few months and helped around the house, in exchange for the reduced rent."

Margherita didn't say anything, just nodded and quietly agreed as she tried comforting her daughter who desperately wanted to attend school to escape the constant criticisms Tessie made about her, her mother and all that was wrong with women who wanted to act like men and study.

Federico's school was one block away from the apartment.

That one block became an obstacle course he had to learn to manage every day, never knowing who would decide on that particular day to suddenly slap him on the face or to take a wet umbrella and swing it behind his legs until his knees buckled and he'd fall to the ground. Tessie had gotten word from Rhoda, the lady who sat on one of the stoops of a nearby building, smoking cigarettes, drinking from tiny bottles she kept in her purse and who would occasionally disappear in cars with men that pulled up in front of her building, "That little white boy of yours is getting his ass kicked again."

Tessie was furious.

"You're like a girl! You gotta get along with them! It's your name! You are in America now. From now on when someone asks your name you say, Freddy, not Federico. What the hell kinda name is that anyway? That's what you tell your teachers too."

Then, she gave him a handful of pennies to offer his tormentors as bribes. But the next day, Federico approached the biggest kid he could find and offered him the money in exchange for protection. It worked. Every day Federico went home in search of more pennies, often working for Tessie to get them.

"There, take this," Tessie ordered as she handed him industrial sized bottles of Pine-Sol and ammonia. "I do for you, you do for me," as she handed him the loose change in her pocket. "Go mop the stairs and when you are done, hose down the garbage pails. Put some soap in them, maybe that will get the stink out."

The mop was taller than he was and the bucket heavy even when empty. He couldn't lift it when it was filled with water, Pine-Sol and ammonia, so he'd dunk the mop and drag up as much water as it held all the way up to the sixth floor. He'd repeat this at least four more times. After finishing rinsing the garbage pails, he'd take them down to the basement, always following his grandfather's instructions on how to proceed and then quickly toss them in and run out. Sometimes, he would sit on the stoop and watch people. Some of the boys from the building would sit next to him pretending not to see him. Once they asked him if he wanted to go down to the basement with the girl from the third floor. Federico didn't understand why, but then they explained that if he gave her a dime, he'd be able to touch her down there. He told them he would think about it. "But probably not because I only have pennies, and I need those to get to school." They laugh at him and ran down the block, leaving Federico to wonder what they had found so funny.

Most of the time, Federico could be found trailing Tessie around with a shopping cart. She'd walk a few steps ahead of him wearing her fur coat, eyeglasses that made her look like a cat, deep red lipstick and a powdered pink face that stopped just below her double chin. She looked to him like a dressed up Grizzly bear impersonating a clown. Every so often a woman or a man barely able to stand approached her holding a bag, or offering up what was tucked inside their coat, asking whether she was interested in buying whatever item had just been stolen from May's Department store on Fulton Street. She'd look at the items and wave it away if she wasn't interested or say, "I'll give you three."

"C'mon Tee, this is good stuff. Let's do ten," the unsteady person would implore.

"For ten I'll go downtown and buy it from the store. Three or nothing," she'd say, knowing that someone needing a fix was in no condition to negotiate. She always got her price.

One day, they were walking by the A&P Supermarket when she noticed a brown paper bag. Someone had dropped their groceries. It looked like it had been there for a while. She looked inside and said, "Lookie here, there's some mozzarella in here. I'll make you something special when we get home."

That afternoon she cut the hard dry cheese in chunks and dipped them in eggs and then breadcrumbs and fried them. She handed Federico the plateful. They didn't smell right. But she stood there, almost daring him to say no after all the trouble she had gone through preparing them. He ate them and spent the rest of the night vomiting.

Margherita asked him what he had eaten.

"Probably something bad from the school lunch," he whispered without looking at his step-grandmother.

Tessie didn't say a word, but Claudia knew what had happened and looked at her with the deep hatred she had learned to keep just below the surface for fear of what might happen if she spoke up.

The day it happened—the day she did speak up—was a warm, sunny September day in 1970—a lifetime since their arrival. School was about to begin, and Claudia was excited thinking about going to school. She had finished doing all that was expected of her that day and had decided to look out the living room window. She placed a pillow on the ledge to rest her arms on and looked toward the sky, hoping to catch the warmth of the sun. A young man living in the building came out and sat on the stoop. He was a handsome boy of fifteen who mostly kept to himself and wasn't really involved with the goings on in the neighborhood. Claudia had noticed him a few times when he walked in the front of the building and had heard someone call his name from a window above, Juan. He had smiled at her a few times. At first, Claudia had looked away, but then smiled back. It was her own special secret and she had not shared it with anyone. It helped her get through the day, the possibility that Juan would smile at her again.

"My name is Juan," he said nervously.

"I know," Claudia said blushing.

"I don't see you in school," Juan said as he got closer to the window.

"I don't go to school right now," she said, avoiding his eyes, hoping he wouldn't ask why. Then she quickly added, "But I will. Soon, I will."

"We could walk to school together, if you want. I can show you how things work. Maybe even show you some salsa moves during break, in the school yard," he said excitedly, showing her a few steps.

"I would like that. Not sure about the salsa moves, not sure I could even do them," Claudia said, her voice bouncy, unable to hold back the excitement she felt.

"It's easy, I'll show you."

As Juan moved to silent music, Tessie and Federico approached the building. The shopping cart was full, and Federico was having difficulty wheeling it smoothly as it kept getting stuck in the cracks on the sidewalk.

"What the hell do you think you are doing there?" Tessie began to yell, "Get inside! You look like a *puttana* hanging out that window!"

"You are not my mother! You can't talk to me like that! I wasn't doing anything wrong."

"You," Tessie turned to Juan, "never look or speak to her again."

"We were just talking," Juan said softly.

"I bet!" Tessie responded with disgust in her voice.

"I hate you! I hate you! *Vacca*!" Claudia finally erupted.

Federico stopped at the bottom of the stoop, his hands bloodless as he clasped the handle of the cart. Claudia was now crying uncontrollably. She dashed inside and Federico dragged the cart up the stoop, parked it in front of his grandfather's front door and ran inside to his sister. Claudia was at the kitchen table sobbing, unable to catch her breath. Tessie stormed in, slamming the door behind her with a force that almost ripped it off its hinges.

"You hate me? After all I've done for you and your mother! You call me a cow in front of that animal? How dare you, I give you everything you have, and this is what I get in return?"

"Don't play the innocent grandmother with me! I know what you say about us, about my mother!"

As she spewed those words Margherita walked in. "What happened!?" she asked.

"Your daughter disrespected me. She yelled at me like trash in the street! After all I've done."

"Apologize to your grandmother," Margherita said as she looked down at her shaken daughter.

"Apologize? My grandmother is dead. She will never take her place. She is just another woman with some money that our grandfather picked up. I will not say sorry! You have no idea all the things she has been saying. She treats us like slaves. It wasn't true I couldn't go to school. She made that up. She keeps me here and turned me into her cleaning lady, laundress and cook! She called me a *puttana*! She tells everyone that we were better off being put in orphanages to be raised right. That you are a whore and you got what you deserved. That our father left us because you sleep with every man you see and that's what you did in Italy, even with his brothers!"

"Did you really say those things?" Margherita said, stunned, turning to Tessie. "Why? Why would you? I thought you really cared for us."

Federico looked at his step-grandmother and saw the blood drain from her face. She put her right hand on her heart and raised the other to the sky and loudly proclaimed, "If I said any of those things that came out of her filthy mouth, may God strike me dead right here! Right now!"

As Tessie uttered the last word, one hand on her heart and the other raised toward heaven, she collapsed of a massive heart attack.

She spent several weeks in hospital. Their grandfather made daily trips bringing soup and whispering sweet-nothings as he gently prodded her to reveal the location of the bank books and the key to the safe, "just in case anything happens." She'd stare at the ceiling, feigning pain and when he got home, he'd turn the apartment upside down as he yelled at God, "Take her! Take her! Why don't you just take that *strega*?!"

Tessie survived, but refused to ever speak to any of them again. Shortly thereafter, she left to stay with her daughter and recuperate, leaving the family to fend for themselves and instructions for them not to be there when she returned. Their grandfather attempted to make amends, but when he realized that his life with her would be a hell worse than the hell it had been, he decided to leave. He caught the next cruise sailing from New York to Genoa, hoping to have better luck with the next wealthy American widow who fell for his charm.

On the day before Federico and Claudia placed the final X on the final page of their calendar, Margherita told them it would be better for them to stay a while longer. They'd have more opportunity here. And the good news was, they would move to a spacious and airy apartment, a much better apartment, and the boarder whom she had met only months before, would help them move. It all made so much sense.

It took less than a year for the divorce to become final. Then Margherita married the man she'd only known for months, but who had been by her side when it all seemed impossible. When he proposed he promised that he would help take care of her and the children; he hoped that she could find a place in her heart for him too. It wasn't love, but Margherita accepted.

Federico and Claudia put the calendar in a photo album that held images of them and their mom. Images that included Margherita's youth, when her dreams were plentiful and hope impatiently waited to make those dreams come true.

They'd been in America one year. That one year had cemented who Federico and Claudia would become as adults. Fear would be their guide, keeping them alerted to anyone wanting to hurt or use them. They would search for love to make them whole, but they could never trust anyone again. Only fools did that—fools didn't know any better. They would be suspicious of every smile on someone's lips, every twinkle in someone's eyes, and every "I love you" they heard. They would demand perfection from themselves and from others, not realizing they had already set themselves up to fail.

Many years later, the two siblings made a trip back to Genoa. Standing side by side, they looked up at the nine-story building, remembering how so many years before they had stood on the balcony of their top-floor apartment imagining the magical things they would do when they arrived in the United States. Perhaps they would even meet Annette, the Mouseketeer that had given them the most hope.

Federico watched his sister as she carefully slipped the calendar out of her purse. The pages had almost disintegrated, you could still see the colorful flowers Claudia had drawn, but the frayed orange yarn no longer held together their dreams from the past. They looked at each other, without saying anything. Neither whispered, "What if?"

Their parents were long gone and now all Federico could do was think of that morning, the day before Thanksgiving.

He had awoke to the smell of toast—but not the old smell of regular toast. A new, incredibly enticing smell. He peered over the arm of his single reclining bed to see his father making breakfast. He walked into the kitchen. His father was spreading butter on toast and signaled to him to sit at the table. Then he heard delicate footsteps, and his mother appeared in the doorway of the kitchen, leaning her head against the jamb lovingly as if she were placing her head on a soft pillow, and as she wrapped her robe tight around her, she exhaled, needing this quiet existence to be the rest of her life. His father reached for his hand. He took it as he ate the toast. He then saw his father's gaze turn toward his mother. His parents were looking in a mirror. She smiled, he smiled. And for a moment the world was perfect.

Favola

Valentina sat in a room at the back of the *sartoria* with two older women whose heads were bowed down as they concentrated on the shirts they held, sewing carefully with needles and thread. Paolo had seen her through the slightly parted curtains as he was being fitted for a new suit. He had not been able to take his eyes off of her.

As Antonio, his tailor, seesawed his itchy handlebar mustache—an adornment belonging to another era—he was unable to hold back a thunderous sneeze at the precise moment that he inserted a needle deep into the shoulder pad of the jacket Paolo was being measured for, accidentally going beyond the fabric and pricking Paolo's skin. He jumped back, expecting Paolo to yell. There was no reaction from Paolo, though—either to the sneeze or to the pricking of his skin. Antonio looked at Paolo and understood why.

"She's taken," Antonio whispered. He continued measuring, making sure no blood had stained the fabric. Paolo seemed oblivious to his words and any pain he may have felt. "I've never seen a girl more beautiful," he said as if talking to himself.

The young woman lifted her head and snuck a bite of

focaccia she had hidden under the sewing counter. Her eyes caught his. "My...che bel ragazzo!" she whispered. "Who is he?" she asked the woman sitting next to her.

"That's Signor Deluca's son, Paolo. He doesn't come in too often. His mother must have insisted on a new suit for Easter. She treats him as if he's twelve, from what I hear. They are one of Genoa's richest families. Finish eating and keep working before Antonio sees you."

He looks like a character in a romance novel, the young woman thought. Then, realizing she was still staring as Paolo, she quickly lowered her gaze and swallowed the salty, soft, rosemary-infused focaccia she had eaten almost every day since first discovering it on her arrival in Genoa at the Principe train station only a year before. She wiped her hands and picked up a needle. Paolo was still looking at her. She confidently held it up ready to thread it, but she missed the eye. She tried again, her hand now trembling a bit. I wish he'd stop looking at me, she thought, beginning to feel self-conscious.

Paolo continued trying to catch her eye, but she was now absorbed as she slowly threaded the needle and began sewing the collar of the shirt she held. Her movements hypnotized him; they were elegant, smooth and focused, like those of a seasoned ballerina practicing her port de bras.

Antonio had picked up on the exchange and quickly finished up his work.

"Mr. Deluca..." Antonio began.

"That's my father, Antonio. Call me Paolo. How many times do I have to tell you, no formalities."

"Okay, Paolo. The suit will be ready before the holiday."

"That's fantastic, I know it's late in the season. I couldn't get away from work. My father keeps sending me to Milan for business."

"We have plenty of time to get it done for you, it's never a problem. We'll see you soon, then?" Antonio said.

Paolo didn't respond. He just stood there. The pause was becoming awkward. Paolo wanted to find a way to ask Antonio about the girl. Perhaps even engage her in conversation—a remark about her beautiful auburn hair? Her bright round hazel eyes? Instead, he found himself being guided toward the front door, barely hearing Antonio asking him to give his regards to his parents and how wonderful it was to see him again.

Paolo walked slowly to his car, parked across the street from the shop, and sat on the hood. It was a red convertible Aston Martin, a present from his parents for his twenty-fourth birthday. He knew it screamed of *figlio di papa*—but he wasn't a spoiled-rich-boy. He had few vices, and cars were his passion. The war's effects were still very much evident in 1951 and Genoa was not a metropolis like Rome or Milan. Few could afford such luxuries. But Paolo had been obsessed with the car since he first laid his eyes on it outside of the casino in Sanremo.

"It's magnificent!" he'd said as his father waited for their chauffeur to arrive.

"It's a good-looking machine. But red? A bit garish, wouldn't you say?" his father noted.

Without having to ask, his parents presented it to him the morning of his birthday, making him promise not to speed.

"You know that if you do, we will find out," his mother had warned. Being an only child, he was watched over by his mother from near or far. Paolo could sometimes swear he was being followed—he wasn't entirely wrong.

At closing time, the seamstresses pushed out of the tailor shop door, chatting about having to go grocery shopping, or having to pick up kids from their grandparent's houses. As they exited Paolo pretended to read a newspaper. The women hurried toward their destinations. Finally, Valentina appeared.

"Ciao, I'll see you tomorrow," she said, waving back at Antonio.

"Looks like rain," he yelled back. "Hurry to catch the tram."

She saw Paolo begin to walk toward her. She began striding down the street at a quick pace, fumbling nervously to wrap her foulard over her head. Her fingers were unable to hold the silky fabric, and when she tried to tie the two ends under her chin, suddenly it flew out of her hands, snagged by a gust of wind. Paolo was right behind her and caught it.

"Signorina, here you are," he said, handing it to her.

"Thank you," she said quietly, cautiously taking the foulard and wrapping it around her hand as if bandaging a wound.

"Signorina, I know you don't know me, but you can ask Antonio about me, my family, I mean," he said quickly. "I am not a lunatic. I just want to get to know you. My name is Paolo Deluca. May I ask your name?"

"I'm engaged," she said.

He chuckled. "I know," he said, "But you must also have

a name?"

She smiled. "Of course I do," she said as she tried to move away.

"Do you like focaccia, Signorina?" he asked out of the blue.

"Yes, I do, but…"

"Where are you from? I hear a slight accent."

She looked down at her hands and blushed.

"I'm from Apulia," she said, almost apologetically. "But I've been here over a year. And I work," she added defensively.

"What town in Apulia?" Paolo said cheerfully, attempting to lighten the moment. "I've vacationed there with my parents; the beaches are stunning."

She interrupted, "I don't think this is a good idea, speaking like this on the street." Slowly enunciating each word, she added, "I don't know you." She began to move away.

Paolo swayed back and forth, wanting to move toward her, but then suddenly he heard his father's voice in his head saying, "Women are to be cherished and respected, not hunted down like game. Always be a gentleman!" Unsure of what to do he blurted, "I will bring you the best focaccia in Genoa. It's from Montaldo's. It's been there forever. My grandparents met there. You will love it!"

"There's really no need," she said as she walked away. Then she stopped and gave a quick glance back. "My name is Valentina," she said, unfurling the foulard and finally wrapping it around her head.

She then walked quickly across Via Balbi and disappeared

into the crowd.

Paolo stood there long after he could no longer see her, oblivious to fact that the rain had begun and the folding roof of his prized Aston Martin was still down.

Paolo had been in Milan for two weeks and the moments of his first encounter with Valentina had played over and over in his head. When his business was finally finished, instead of driving directly to Genoa he took a detour to Recco, to Montaldo's, to pick up focaccia for Valentina. He wanted to get there when it opened. Paolo looked at his watch. Five forty-five in the morning. He couldn't remember the last time he'd been up that early. Venice, he smiled. His senior year at university. The Carnival. He'd been invited to a ball hosted by one of his father's business associates. On his arrival, Paolo was introduced to the man's daughter, Laura—they immediately understood why they were brought together; a merger between their families would result in a very powerful alliance. They played along for a bit, feigning a deep conversation while her parents looked on. Satisfied, they moved on to mingle with their other guests while Paolo and Laura melted in the crowd in search of other masked strangers. Paolo remembered being somewhere close to St. Mark's Square the next morning and hearing the bell tower strike six as he fell asleep next to a woman in a Marie Antoinette costume whose face he couldn't recall. There had been so many girls since then, all sweet—but not necessarily looking for love, rather in search of someone who could provide them with a luxurious life.

He looked at his watch again and then up at the sign, Panificio Montaldo, waiting for the doors to open. His grandparents had met here. They had not seen eye to eye on much during their marriage, but the one thing they always agreed on was that this bakery made the best focaccia with crescenza cheese anywhere in Liguria.

Once the purchase was made, he rushed back to Genoa so the focaccia would still be warm when he got there. He pulled up outside of Finollo's and looked to see if Valentina had arrived. He saw no one except for Antonio. He walked in the shop holding the package of focaccia wrapped in wax paper and tied together with a white string.

"Antonio, has Valentina come in yet? I happened to be in Recco, I drove by Montaldo and thought I know how much she likes focaccia and…"

He trailed off as Antonio looked at him holding the package. He felt foolish. He'd been phoning the shop every day hoping to speak to Valentina. When Antonio picked up, it seemed she was always running an errand. But on those rare times when Antonio happened to be out and someone else answered, he was able to speak to her.

At first Valentina kept the conversations short, always ending them by saying, "I have to get back to work, I don't think we should be talking like this, it feels wrong." But after a few times speaking to him she would move quickly to take the call before Antonio came back. She enjoyed their talks, even when they were composed only of discussions of the weather.

"Paolo," Antonio began slowly, as he took out his pocket watch, an heirloom from the past that would soon become fashionable again because the Hollywood actor, James Dean, considered it a lucky charm. Antonio often used it as a prop, something to look at to avoid someone's eyes when he was about to have an uncomfortable conversation. "I know you and your family a very long time, I feel I can be candid. What I want to say to you now comes from a place of respect."

Paolo looked down at his hands holding the package, sure of what was coming next.

"This girl," Antonio continued, "is from a small town. She lost both her parents and had no place to go. I asked her here to work. She met a nice young man and now is living with his family until he can save enough for the wedding."

"I only wanted to bring her focaccia," Paolo said apologetically.

"All you will do is confuse her. You are a gentleman from a noble family. She is a sweet girl from a working family. Valentina has nothing in common with you and your world. And I'm sure you realize that your parents would never accept a union between the two of you—never. Besides, she is spoken for, you know that. Just let this one go."

Paolo placed the package down on the counter, looking around the shop searching for a lifeline. As he headed to the door, he stopped.

"Wait!" Paolo suddenly said. "You just said you know me a long time. You know everything about me and my family. Have I ever disrespected or intentionally hurt anyone, especially young ladies?"

"No, but..." Antonio said, having now put his pocket watch away but still wanting to avoid Paolo's eyes. He began unfolding a bolt of fabric on the cutting table, pretending to take measurements.

"Then give me one day. I only want to spend a few hours alone with her and just talk. I promise. I give you my word, I won't hurt her."

"Some promises are difficult to keep. But you are giving me your word and that's worth much more."

"Grazie! Grazie! Really! Thank you, Antonio," Paolo yelled like a child opening up a Christmas present while heading to the door. "I'll call you. Please make sure she gets the focaccia"

A few days later, Valentina arrived early at Finollo. The door was open, but there was no sign of Antonio. He was probably at the café for his usual espresso and cornetto. He would bring one back for Valentina along with a cappuccino. Her favorite part of the crunchy sweet croissant was dunking it in her cappuccino and letting it melt in her mouth.

Antonio had always been good to her family. His brother, Ignazio, had taught Valentina how to sew back in her hometown. He was the master tailor in town and everyone referred to him as "Maestro." Valentina had never liked going to school, preferring to read hours on end under the shade of the huge fig tree behind her family's home. She attended school only on those days when the fascist soldiers provided lunches for the children. Otherwise, she much preferred her books over the noisy, overcrowded school room. It was an escape from the poverty and constant hunger that the war had brought on.

Valentina's mother had been close friends with Antonio and Ignazio, they had grown up together in the small village. The two brothers came from a long line of tailors. Antonio, already a highly skilled tailor in his early twenties, decided to try his luck in the north. He left for Genoa and found work as an apprentice at Finollo, the premiere tailor shop in the city. He quickly became *il capo sarto*, while Ignazio, a more timid and reserved type, preferred the familiarity of home and chose to stay behind and teach.

Since school had no appeal for Valentina, she decided to take Ignazio up on his offer to study under him. She was the youngest in the group and enjoyed sitting around in a circle sewing with the women, listening to their gossip, their assertions becoming murmurs when the news became too indelicate for Valentina to hear. As the women giggled and teased, Ignazio's eyes scanned the room, making sure his standards were met. He understood early on that Valentina had promise, she would become an accomplished seamstress. And quickly, she became his favorite.

A few years after the war ended Valentina had found herself alone. Her mother had died. They called it a stroke, but Valentina knew it to be a broken heart. Her brothers, Gianni and Renaldo, were among the first to join the Resistance against the Nazi and Fascist occupation. Their efforts were thwarted when a neighbor gave their location away to Nazi soldiers in exchange for a kilo of flour. Gianni and Renaldo were arrested and without any due process were shot in the piazza along with five other teenagers for all the townspeople to witness, including Valentina's mother, who never spoke another word after that moment.

Valentina's father, a barber, was found dead on his wife's grave soon after. A note in his pocket read, "Life is unbearable for me…forgive me." He had slashed his own throat with his razor.

Ignazio had known Valentina all her life and had seen her grow into a ravishing beauty constantly being chased by the young men in town. He had made a promise to her mother to look after her. "There is too much sadness here for you," he told her. "Since the war ended, little has changed here. I think it would be better for you to go up north, to work and make a life for yourself."

"You're right. I can't keep living under my sister's roof. She has her own family to look after and there's not enough to go around," said Valentina.

Meanwhile, Antonio had never stopped working, even during the war. "The rich never stop being rich," he wrote in a letter to Ignazio. "They still want their suits and shirts made by hand even as a war is being fought around them." Ignazio had kept his brother informed of all the happenings in their hometown, and asked Antonio to secure a position for Valentina so that she could start a new life somewhere where the reminders of her parents and brothers weren't constantly present.

Shortly after, Ignazio purchased a one-way train ticket to Genoa for Valentina.

Ignazio and Valentina stood on the platform, peering down the tracks, looking for the train to appear from beyond the horizon. Valentina wore a gray wool coat she had received from an aunt who had, many years before the war, emigrated to the United States. It was more suited to a mature woman, but it was warm and she appreciated it. Her dress was one left behind by her mother. Ignazio couldn't do anything about the coat but he had lovingly altered the dress to reflect the style of a dress Valentina had admired in *Grazia*, a glamour magazine for ladies that featured the fashions of the day along with a popular advice column written by Donna Letizia, whom everyone thought was a Contessa. In reality she was a he, an editor of the magazine. Her, or rather, his words, were gospel for many women—everything from how to know you were in love to greeting guests to your home for a dinner party. Valentina read it religiously. She was determined to better herself in every aspect of life.

They waited silently—everything having been said. Valentina's lone suitcase beside her, her hands in her coat pockets, one clenching the scrap of paper with Antonio's address in Genoa. "In case he can't make the train or if you get lost," Ignazio had said, placing it in the palm of her hand.

Ignazio shifted side to side, feeling—what? Uncomfortable, he thought. He wore a pinstripe suit that Antonio had sent to him years before, saying that it had never been picked up by its owner. Ignazio altered it to fit him and wore it only on special occasions. The train station was a ten-minute walk from the town's piazza where he had rendezvoused with Valentina but he wanted to look nice, he felt it was an important moment in the young woman's life and she should remember it as such. He felt anxious or was it envy? Why would he be envious? He knew he could never leave this small town. It was his home but more importantly it was his safe heaven. No one spoke about his condition and the townspeople were respectful enough even if he could never completely be himself among them. He had been freer at some point in his life, when he was much younger. He'd been hopeful of having a fuller life, a life he could share with a man, someone who would love him. But those dreams were shelved when the Fascist regime took power. Ignazio had heard of the island in Termi where men like him were being shipped to by order of Mussolini. Once you were branded a *femminnella*—a little girl—your life was no longer your own. He was terrified of being shipped there. He'd slowly retreated in a world of invisible beings hiding in their homes, men afraid to go out for fear of being taken away never to be seen again. Once the war began, the island project was disbanded and the men, now publicly known to be homosexuals, were released back into society to live their lives in hiding for fear of being killed by their own countrymen.

Like Ignazio, Valentina had never left her little town of Locorotondo, a picturesque town brimming with blinding white colored limestone Trulli homes with stone tiled cone-roofs that gave it a quaint, storybook feel, especially in the winter when rare snow falls covered the cobblestone streets and dotted the gray stone roofs. It was for Valentina all she needed until the day she found herself alone. With her parents and brothers gone and her sister having a family of her own, Valentina knew the town no longer had a place for her.

When the train finally arrived, it brought with it a thunderous rumbling sound that momentarily quieted the loud beating echoing in Valentina's ears which began days before— the moment she had realized that once she stepped on that train, she would truly be on her own and alone.

Ignazio once again went over all the train changes, she had to make; Locorotondo to Putignano, Putignano to Bari Central, Bari Central to Rome Termini, Rome Termini to Genoa Piazza Principe. It would take about sixteen hours and she was only to ask information from train conductors and she should try and find a seat next to a family or an elderly lady. His eyes were filled with tears when she boarded. "Vai, vai… Mi raccomando, stai alerta."

"Yes, I'll be careful and I will definitely stay alert," Valentina replied, unable to hold back her own tears. On seeing her cry, Ignazio quickly turned and walked away without saying another word, one hand up in the air gesturing goodbye while the other reached for a handkerchief in his pocket.

Valentina luckily found a seat near a window on each train. Her neck ached from constantly twisting as she looked out at the farmland and towns whizzing by. Having had very little sleep the week before, she kept dozing off with her temple glued to the window. At times she snapped awake with her head dangling back and forth from her shoulders to the rhythm of the train's movement. Finally, when she heard the conductor announce, "Next stop, Genoa, Principe," her heart began to race and she made a dash for the washroom to freshen up and then returned to make sure she would not miss anything. The train slowed down and began rolling toward its final stop as if in slow motion. To the left of the train all she could see from her seat was the sea, the sun glinting over the waves creating a welcoming, sparkled carpet that made Valentina break out in a bittersweet smile. Mom had always wanted to see Genoa, she thought.

The train passed tall gray stone buildings, once considered elegant and now inhabited by families sharing many of the flats because of the lack of housing after the war. Clotheslines drooped from window to window drying undergarments, shirts, and housedresses that, like the old buildings, had seen better days. Some structures sat next to mounds of crumbled stones where another building had stood. Children stood by large open windows and balconies waving to unseen strangers arriving on the train. Valentina looked beyond the buildings seeing the majestic mountains above Genoa, once again, thinking of her mother and how happy she would been to also see this. Valentina was not naïve, she knew that this city had been changed by the war and these people had suffered and lost like so many others, but in this moment, just for this moment she needed to hope that like in the *favolas*, the fables, she had read as a child, her own story in this place would have a happy ending.

She picked Antonio out from the crowd immediately. Unlike Ignazio, who was tall and thin and whose face was rectangular, Antonio was shorter, stout, with a round sweet face resembling a cherub—his signature handlebar mustache waxed and shiny. The one thing the two brothers shared and which made them unmistakenly brothers were their eyes—they were identical; almond-shaped with a soft chestnut color that in the sunlight seemed to turn a deep silky honey color.

"My brother was right; you are a beauty. You remind me so much of your mom—rest her soul." Antonio glanced upwards, making the sign of the cross, and Valentina followed his gaze half expecting to actually see her mother above them. When Antonio lifted her suitcase, he reacted with a questioning look—it was very light. It only contained a few items: a housedress, undergarments, a pajama, a pair of worn slippers and the few photographs of her family.

"I didn't have much to pack." Valentina said, blushing.

"We'll take care of everything, *piccola mia*. Don't worry, it's all going to be fine. Welcome to Genoa! The wounds are still healing, it's going to take a bit more time, but soon it will be back to her old self."

They stepped out of the train station. After breathing the stale air on the train for so many hours she welcomed the light cool breeze. The sun was shining and the warmth felt good on her skin. Antonio handed her a brown paper bag. "Here, you must be hungry, it's focaccia, just out of the oven, it's still warm. Genoa has the best focaccia in Italy. It's unlike any other."

Valentina opened the bag and inhaled the scent—it embraced her with a familiar scent like that of the bread her mother baked in the wood-burning oven built in their garden decades before by her grandfather. She took a bite and tasted the crispy bread that thinned out in areas with round grooves drizzled with olive oil, water and sprinkled with salt. I'm in love, Valentina thought. She suddenly hugged Antonio. He wrapped his arms around her.

"I'm glad you are here," Antonio said holding back tears.

"I know my mother would want to thank you. And I thank you. It's all very beautiful, I know I'm going to be happy here."

As Valentina waited for Antonio to return, she looked around the shop, something she always did when she wasn't in the sewing room, scrutinizing every corner of the establishment, running her hand over the shiny counters, opening small drawers filled with brass buttons or small colorful soft swatches collected through the years. The shop had been there since the 1880s and its original owner, Emanuele Finollo, had designed everything, from the front door to the furniture, counters, and lamps in art nouveau style. Every time Valentina walked in, it was as if she was going back in time, entering a past of beauty and elegance—impenetrable. "One day," she had told Antonio, "I want to have a home that looks just like this shop."

Antonio came in holding the cornetto and a cappuccino, "Here you go, enjoy."

"Thank you," Valentina smiled and began to go toward the sewing room.

"Where is everybody?" she asked.

"Valentina, today there is no sewing. I have a lot of paperwork to attend to, fabrics to order, payments to make, the accountant wants to go over the books so I will need to concentrate. I gave everyone the day off," he said, "with pay, of course."

Valentina looked lost. "I can still work. I won't make any noise, and if there are fittings to do, I can look after customers," she offered.

"I am going to need total silence and I need to be alone. Go and see a bit of the city, you've been working practically every day since you got here. Besides, we'll be going into sewing for the fall season and working very long hours. Take advantage of this. Go!" Antonio said.

Valentina, finished her cappuccino, wrapped the cornetto in paper, placed it in her purse and headed toward the door. "Fine, if you insist," she said unexcitedly and walked out of the shop.

Paolo was standing across the street. This time Valentina didn't hurry away. Instead, she looked back at Antonio standing in the shop. He smiled and nodded his head in approval.

"Did you enjoy the focaccia?" Paolo said.

"Yes, thank you. It was very good. It was the first time I had focaccia from Recco," she replied.

They stood awkwardly looking around. Though they'd spoken on the phone, they hadn't seen each other since the first day they'd met.

"Antonio had mentioned that he would be closing for the day and I thought since you were going to have the day off it might be nice to take a ride along the coast. Lunch in Portofino perhaps," Paolo said, sounding rehearsed.

"I see," said Valentina. "So you just happened to speak to Antonio, and you figured I'd be here and you want to take me to lunch in Portofino?"

"Yes, that's how it happened," Paolo said, avoiding her eyes and looking down at his jacket, brushing off invisible lint with his hands.

"It all sounds like a silly plan concocted in a romance novel, but since I have the day off, and I know it's only going to be lunch, let's go!" she said as she headed toward the car. Paolo ran ahead, opened the passenger door, looked across the street and gave Antonio, who was still standing inside the shop looking at them, a thumbs up.

Valentina slowly slid into the plush seat. The top was down and the early morning sun had warmed the soft brown leather; it felt like a warm embrace. She wasn't sure what she should do with her hands but then noticed the strap on the side of the windshield frame and immediately reached for it, holding tightly. Her other hand held the single handle of her black faux leather bag and with her back straight, she focused straight ahead. Paolo walked around to his side of the car and smiled as he watched Valentina ready herself for the ride. Instead of opening his own door, Paolo sprang over it. Valentina didn't move except to raise her eyebrows, press her lips together and raise her chin, signaling that she wasn't impressed. Paolo laughed as he started the car and said, "This is going to be a wonderful afternoon, you'll see."

Neither said a word as Paolo skillfully zigzagged in and out of traffic, making his way through the city toward Via Aurelia, the main avenue that hugs the coastline connecting the small communes along the Riviera di Levante.

The wind billowed through Valentina's hair as she tried to keep it from whipping her face by rotating her head side to side. When she realized it was in vain, she let go of the strap and pulled out a foulard. Struggling against the wind, she attempted to wrap her head. After the third try, she gave up, rolled the silk fabric into a ball and instead of placing it back into her purse she reached for the glove compartment. As she opened it, she noticed a lipstick and held it up to Paolo. "Nice shade of red," she said loudly.

"It's my mom's," Paolo said unconvincingly.

"I bet." Valentina retorted as she tossed the lipstick and foulard into the glove compartment. Then she took her hair and held it with one hand like a ponytail while she once again reached for the strap on the side of windshield's frame.

Once they reached Via Aurelia, the traffic subsided and Paolo finally slowed down. Valentina gazed over, and she relaxed noticing his confidence controlling the little red sport car, one hand on the large wood grain steering wheel and one on the stick shift smoothly changing gears and giving it what it needed to make it purr.

She let the strap go and caressed the side of her seat. The

brown leather felt strong under her skin, and as she rolled her fingers around the red piping that held the fabric together, she wondered what kind of a machine had stitched it together or whether a seamstress had sewn it by hand before dressing the cushions. She looked at the shiny red dashboard with the large round chrome dials and tried figuring out what it all meant. This was her first magic carpet ride, she thought. She felt a sudden sense of power.

Valentina broke the silence. "You always get what you wish for don't you?"

Paolo looked over and said, "Not always. Right now I wish I was sitting next to someone who was not engaged, yet I am sitting next to a friend who thinks me a spoiled brat."

Valentina laughed.

They turned off Via Aurelia and began winding down the steep road that snakes around the side of the hill heading down toward Portofino. The road was so narrow that Valentina could almost touch the bougainvillea creeping across the side of the rocky hillside. She looked out at the sea and the villas that sat like royalty, seeming as if they expected to be fawned over.

"Beautiful, aren't they?" Paolo said.

"Yes, magnificent, but there's such a sadness to them. They look unlived in, lonely in a strange way."

"They probably are lonely since most of the people who own them have left for Cortina. It's skiing season, you know," Paolo said.

"Yes, of course, skiing season. *Che testa vuota!* What an

airhead! I guess I missed it this year!" Valentina said with a girlish giggle. Then with more anger in her voice that she'd intended, "Silly of me! Here I am sewing shirts day in and day out, my fingers stiff at night, while I should have been on the Alps practicing my skiing."

"I'm sorry, I didn't mean…" Paolo said, suddenly realizing how pretentious he'd sounded.

"No need to be," Valentina said, regretting her outburst and knowing he hadn't meant anything by it. She was angry at herself for showing her insecurities and resentment toward a world she yearned for but had clearly not been part of and might never be.

Paolo looked over at her. "I'm an idiot, don't be angry," he said softly.

But Valentina didn't say anything; she was looking toward the sea, holding back tears. She didn't want to seem weak. I'm the damn idiot, she thought. Why did I agree to this?

They drove in silence until Paolo, unsure of what he should do or say, turned the radio on. Nilla Pizzi, the recent winner of Sanremo Music Festival, was singing that year's winning song, "Thank You for the Flowers." Valentina excitedly turned up the volume. "Such a beautiful song! She deserved to win," she said as she began humming along. She looked at Paolo, who seemed to be waiting for some sort of sign from her. She smiled at him. You are a handsome man, Mr. Deluca, she thought, very handsome—I wonder how many girls you've swept off their feet.

Paolo parked and turned off the engine. They sat for a moment and then he reached over and took Valentina's hands, kissing them. "I'm so happy you are here. Let's enjoy this beautiful place. He held her hands until she slowly pulled them away.

"I'm happy I came," she said. "Don't spoil me, though. I may get used to it." She laughed getting out of the car.

In town, they strolled the cobblestone walkways, the narrow winding roads lined with stone houses painted pastel colors. Paolo walked with hands clasped behind him, like a patient tour guide, or a contemplative monk. Valentina followed at a distance, taking in the view as it peeked out from behind the houses and trees. Neither had said a word since their exchange in the car. Along the waterfront, an old man fished while mewling cats circled him waiting for the innards from gutted fish. Then they climbed a narrow lane leading up a steep hill, at the top of which, were the steps of the Church of Saint George.

The modest chapel was surrounded by scaffolding. There were a few men carefully plastering on the side and a few workers slowly painting the facade a mellow amber color that contrasted the deep green wooden doors donning six rectangle panels carved with depictions of various religious historical scenes.

"It's still being repaired. It was bombed during the war," Paolo said dryly, commenting without saying anything more.

Valentina walked toward the front doors.

"Signorina, la chiesa e chiusa," one of the workers warned.

"They keep it closed for now until they are sure it's safe to go in," Paolo confirmed.

There was something about this church that reminded Valentina of the church in her home hometown of Locorotondo. She had learned to keep her feelings at bay—if a memory of her parents or her brothers appeared in her mind, she willed it away, refusing to think of details or allowing it to replay like a harsh punishment—but in this instant, looking at this church her emotions took over and tears began to stream down her face. She allowed them to flow so as not to scream and then quickly she wiped them away and made the sign of the cross.

When she turned to face Paolo, his back was to her and he was standing motionless looking out at the Ligurian Sea as the sun caressed the slow undulating waves. As she approached Paolo, Valentina couldn't help but notice how tall he was, his square shoulders and the neat hairline just above the rim of his shirt. She had an overwhelming need to wrap her arms around him and kiss his neck.

"Thank you for bringing me here. It's the most beautiful place I've ever been to."

When he turned, they were face to face, their breaths meeting like an electric wave. He took a step back and cleared his throat. "You are welcome," Paolo said, happy to see her smile but avoiding what he really wanted to express. "We have time before my friend, Carlo, opens his trattoria. His wife makes the best food on the Riviera."

He invited her to sit on a nearby bench as he regaled her

with the history of the town and of the region of Liguria like a school teacher lecturing his pupils on a school trip. Valentina would now and then interject an, "Oh I didn't know that," or "That's very interesting," as he rattled off dates, names and events. Once he'd run out of things to say he sat quietly next to her not looking at the view, but rather focused on Valentina.

"You are truly the most beautiful woman I've ever met. I wish I had met you sooner," he said.

He is going to kiss me, Valentina thought. I should move. I should stop him, I should... but as the thought dissolved, not reaching the place where all right decisions live but one day, when it's too late, are ultimately regretted, he took her in his arms and kissed her, deeply, with a need that had somehow taken a hold of them on the day their eyes met, when perhaps, not understanding why, all their doubts vanished and every-thing became crystal clear. The moment when the word *love* becomes just a word in songs and stories but has nothing to do with truth and with the sense of totality felt by two connected people who always knew that the other existed somewhere in the world.

Their lips parted, neither of them moving, they just sat there, both feeling like a huge weight had been lifted and they could now breathe easier. Valentina looked up at Paolo and suddenly as if someone had just spilled a bucket of ice water over her head, she pulled away. My God! she thought, Did I just kiss this man? She felt her legs giving away and so as not to faint she steadied herself on the back rest of the bench. She quickly straightened up and said, "It's close to lunch time.

Shall we go?" She moved away and walked toward the descent of the hill as if neither the kiss or her realization had happened, leaving Paolo to also wonder whether it had really taken place. He followed.

They began the steep descent. Valentina walked slowly, close to the side, reaching for whatever she could hold on to so as not to slip and fall. Paolo, who was now ahead of her, turned and offered his hand.

"I don't want you to get hurt, Antonio will have my head." She hesitated.

She took his hand. For a moment they did not move. Valentina then took his arm. He placed his hand over hers. Neither spoke. The only other times that Valentina had been this close to a man was while dancing. Even her fiancée had only held her hand. They had never been alone together and she did not know what it meant to be close to a man. Now, someone was holding her up, making sure she would not fall, making sure she was protected. She squeezed a little tighter. Paolo was certain he could feel her heart was racing. And he was glad.

Carlo greeted them with open arms. He was a short round man with a significant round face with very red cheeks who if dressed in a colorful sarafan, would surely resemble a babushka doll.

"Carissimo!" he said to Paolo as he hugged him and kissed him on both cheeks. He took Valentina's hand and kissed it. "Welcome! Please make yourselves comfortable. It's not terribly cold today, I have a table ready outside so you can take in the splendor of the sea. And I also have chilled bottle of our local wine, a Vermentino that will go very well with most of the dishes on our menu. Signorina, would you like to see a menu now?"

Valentina nodded, but then looked at Paolo.

"Carlo," said Paolo, "I would suggest whatever you have on special today. Valentina, do you agree?"

"Yes, that sounds perfect," she replied, relieved. Valentina hadn't been to restaurants except for the occasional pizza and beer on Saturday nights. Paolo had picked up on her discomfort.

"We will start with baked stuffed anchovies, then homemade trofie with pesto, followed by grilled branzino served with mixed grilled vegetables and for dessert lemon tart and a good Amaro to help with the digestion."

When he walked away Valentina chuckled. "Boy, that's a change from my usual." Valentina's midday dinner consisted of focaccia or bread with cheese, or a slice or two of mortadella. Food had been scarce during the war and for many it still was. "It all sounds delicious."

As she ate, Paolo looked at her with great interest. She was in a world all her own, savoring each bite, sometimes closing her eyes as if trying to hold on to the flavors, afraid of forgetting them.

"I know, I know," Valentina said, "I'm not dainty like other girls who pick their food delicately. I can't help it. It's why we are here, right? To eat!" The wine had made her giddy. "Tell me about your family. Where did you live? What do you want to do when you grow up?" Valentina laughed. Paolo smirked.

"I am being molded to follow in my father's footsteps and eventually run Deluca Steel, a company he built and that I had nothing to do with. Steel is not glamourous but it is in demand especially during wartime, and it has given me and my family anything we desire," Paolo said, suddenly serious. "I didn't go to school like other kids until the war ended and only because I insisted, threatening to run away. Eventually I studied economics at university. But I grew up with tutors, I am an only child. During the war I wasn't allowed out of the house. We lived in the country surrounded by fields and nothing else. It was strangely quiet there given that Genoa was being constantly bombarded. No one ever came to visit except for suspicious looking men who'd tiptoe in late at night to talk to my father in his study." Paolo paused, then continued somberly. "I never heard any of their conversations. I know my father is not a political person. He is a pragmatist. Whatever he might have done, he did for the business. It was a marriage of convenience. Every business man in Italy had to make a deal with the devil if they were to survive. He always says that in order to keep things moving you have to walk on a tightrope. My father never talks about the war."

"No one really does. If it didn't bring heartache, then it brought guilt from whatever had to be done to survive it," Valentina said.

"I don't know what to feel. I didn't have a choice. He did, but I can't judge him, it's not my place. Am I complicit? I feel

I am. I know people were starving and dying while I was safe, never missing a meal—would anything have changed had my father chosen to take a different stand? I know he helped in his own way, but always for the greater good—the business."

"There's nothing you could have done then. None of us could—we were puppets," Valentina murmured almost to herself. "Now we have no choice but to suffer the pain of everything we lost."

They both looked out toward the sea.

"Tell me about your family," Paolo said. The mood had changed. Valentina's smile was gone.

"I don't want to think about sad things," she said. "They are packed in tiny sealed boxes and shoved all the way in a tightly shut closet in the back of mind. I am constantly leaning on the door so that it doesn't have a chance to open."

A darkness fell on Valentina's face as if one of the boxes had suddenly burst, releasing some horrible memory that made her entire body tremble for a moment. Paolo wanted to reach out and hold her but was afraid of how she might react. All he could think to say was, "I'm sorry." Then to try to bring her back to this moment he asked, "Can you tell me about your fiancée?"

Valentina looked at Paolo inquisitively, wondering why, of all things he would ask about him.

"He's a nice man. His name is Renato," Valentina said as she took another bite of tart.

"And? How did you meet him? How long have you known him?" Paolo pressed, a bit annoyed at having heard his name and now sorry to have brought up the subject.

"Antonio introduced us at a family party. Renato's family is from a nearby town where I'm from. I'm sure it was all set up—as you know, Antonio likes to do that sort of thing," Valentina said as Paolo lowered his eyes for a moment.

"So, we talked and then he would come to the shop, walk me home, tell me about his goal of becoming a supervisor in the customs office at the docks, how he unloads cargo. It took just a few weeks," Valentina said quietly.

"For him to propose?" Paolo asked.

"Yes, to propose. I thought I had more time. He asked and I said, yes."

Paolo was suddenly interested in knowing more. He saw an opportunity here to widen the gap between Valentina's needs and her true desires. "More time for what? To know if you really loved him?"

Valentina picked up her purse sitting on the floor on the side of her chair motioning her intent to get up from the table. Paolo stopped her by taking her hand.

"We are just talking," he said. "That's what friends do, right?"

Valentina settled and took a sip of the icy cold Amaro. "He asked me to marry him in front of the entire family. How was I going to refuse him? I felt I had no other choice. I was brought there for that reason. Antonio and Ignazio felt it would be best for me to marry. Did anyone ask me what I wanted?" Her voice was sharp and almost shrill as if she'd had wished she'd asked that question the moment of the proposal.

"Then why did you say yes?" Paolo asked as Valentina nervously kept folding her napkin in different shapes.

"I could be more independent."

"By marrying someone you hardly know or love?"

"It's a start," Valentina said. "And it's what's expected, it has to be enough."

"But you have choices, you can wait."

"Right now, no one really has a choice. Not even you. Your life has been set. You will follow in your father's footsteps, and I will marry a nice man whom I will learn to love," Valentina said.

Paolo didn't respond.

"Thank you for the wonderful day and the delicious meal, but it's getting late and I have to get back. I am meeting my fiancée's mother later. She wants to fit me for the wedding dress. It was hers." Valentina slammed the table as she got up and without waiting for Paolo headed toward the car.

"Valentina, wait," Paolo said. "I didn't want to upset you."

"Any girl would be lucky to have you," Valentina said gently.

"Would you have considered it?"

"Paolo, we come from opposite worlds. Even if I said yes, it could never work, you have to see that," Valentina said.

"All I know is that I haven't stopped thinking about you since I first saw you," Paolo said. "I know you like me. You wouldn't be here otherwise. Perhaps I should be happy for that much. After all, I gave my word."

It was obvious that Valentina understood to whom Paolo

had given his word to. "Well then, let's go," she said somewhat disappointed.

They drove back to Genoa, Paolo managing the late afternoon traffic as Valentina gazed down, softly rubbing the small calluses on the sides of her thumb and forefinger. Once back in the city, Valentina asked to be dropped off a few blocks from the tram.

"Valentina, I'm sorry if I've said anything to upset you. I can't help how I feel. Before you go, please tell me I can see you again," Paolo said as he opened the door to the car for her.

She stood looking at him, encouraging him with a smile, but then she shook her head and said, "No". As she opened her door, he reached for the glove compartment where she had placed the foulard but then, on second thought, he pulled his hand back.

"Valentina, *ti prego*, just one kiss." She reached over and placed a soft gentle kiss on his lips, her hand caressing his face as she leaned her cheek on his.

"I wish it could be different. You've always been in my dreams." She then quickly got out of the car and Paolo jumped out and began following her. "Don't," she said without turning around. He stopped and looked at her once again walking away from him.

A young man in a Vespa stopped by Paolo, shouting, "That your car?"

Paolo barely nodded.

"It's fantastic! I bet you get girls falling all over themselves over you."

With an ironic smile on his face Paolo said, "Yeah, sure, I do, all the time."

As he watched Valentina slowly walk away two men strolling by her whistled, "Bella!"

Valentina stopped but didn't turn around. Like a bird she stretched her neck, and with her head high she quickly picked up her step as Paolo watched her once again disappear in the crowd.

※

The next day Valentina burst into the shop looking around. "Anyone here?" she asked a startled Antonio.

"No, not yet. What happened?" he asked. "Are you all right?"

"How could you do that to me, Antonio? Help set up this bizarre rendezvous, you of all people! You introduced me to Renato. You know I'm getting married, why would you do it? Were you testing my devotion to Renato? Were you trying to keep your rich client happy?" Valentina said, close to tears.

"I'm sorry. I really am. Did he do anything out of line?" Antonio asked.

"No, no, he didn't. He was a perfect gentleman, but you know that, and that's why you allowed it. Didn't you consider that I could fall in love? Did you think I would be oblivious to all the things he could give me, knowing I could never have them?" Valentina asked.

"I'm so sorry," Antonio said as he sat behind his desk looking dejected, "I knew that it was probably a bad idea. I didn't know what to do. I thought you should have the choice. I didn't want to take that away from you."

"I know. You've always been fair. I can't deny my interest in him, but it was a fantasy more than anything else—I knew it had to be that. I never thought I would actually spend time with him, alone." Valentina looked around the shop and then examined her hands. "Paolo made me think about my future in a different way. Saying yes to Renato made sense even though I don't love him the way I should. We are two people from the same world with small achievable dreams and perhaps a life with some security, it could work, right? Even without love?" she said.

"Valentina, Renato is a good man."

"And then there's Paolo… didn't take much to fall in love with him. What's not to love? He is handsome, kind, intelligent and let's not forget rich, he could give me everything I ever dreamt of. But he doesn't know life, his parents made sure of that." Valentina's voice was suddenly cold, almost angry. "He lives in a city that was devastated by the war, but doesn't understand what really happened to us. His father collaborated with the scum of the earth. It wasn't Paolo's fault, I know that, and his father did it out of desperation. Many people did things out of desperation. But desperation murdered innocent people including my family. There's no way I could be part of his family. When Paolo looks at me, I almost believe that it could be alright, maybe I could be with him, but then I think to myself, You should know better than that."

"What are you going to do, Valentina?" Antonio

whispered as he saw two junior seamstresses enter the shop.

"I don't really know," Valentina said. She went to her station in the sewing room and sat in her chair looking around her table, lining up the spools of thread seeming to be seeing them all for the first time.

Two months went by. Paolo didn't call or try to see Valentina. Every day she'd leave the shop and look across Via Balbi and then she'd walk across to catch the tram as she'd done so many other times. Despite all the rationalizations she'd issued, she couldn't stop thinking of Paolo. Whenever she heard the intro to "Thank You for the Flowers," her eyes would fill with tears. "What's wrong, Valentina?" her future sister-in-law, Ilaria asked one evening as they cleared the table while the song played on the radio.

"Nothing, nothing, just a bit tired I guess," Valentina replied, letting her emotions show, something she rarely did, especially in front of Ilaria.

"You should be happy. You are getting married soon—having second thoughts?" Ilaria asked suspiciously. She was a woman without a filter, who had worn black since the day the news came of her husband's death in the war—news delivered in an unsealed envelope, his body had never been returned. Perhaps, it was the reason her thin face expressed anger even when she smiled.

"Don't be silly," Valentina said quickly, regaining her composure. "I'm in love after all, what reason would I have to have second thoughts?"

Her fiancée had finally saved enough money.

On a warm, early spring day, Valentina made her way to the tram after work. Antonio had given her the afternoon off so she could meet Ilaria and make final preparations for the wedding that would take place in two days.

She walked slowly as she window shopped along Via Balbi. Many of the windows were dressed for Easter. She stopped in front of a bakery whose window was decorated with a very large chocolate egg wrapped in silver foil held together with a large pink bow and surrounded by dozens of different sized eggs wrapped in light blue, orange, and yellow foils. She closed her eyes for a moment and inhaled the sweet scents coming from the bakery.

She looked at the workers, many of whom had emigrated from the south to help rebuild the city, some struggling as they wheeled barrels of bricks into buildings. Many stopped midway to whistle at Valentina, and some yelled, "Can I take you out tonight?" Valentina gestured with her hand vertically up to her nose, snapped it forward, and said, "You are crazy! Not a chance!" One worker placed his hands on his heart pretending to be wounded.

People around Valentina were moving at a furious pace, women speeding by holding bags of groceries, men sprinting with newspapers tucked under their arms, teenage girls whizzing by arm in arm laughing while Valentina strolled along, sometimes stopping to watch.

A woman yelled as her neighbor was hanging clothes out on the clothesline, "Laundry is put out in the morning to dry, not in the afternoon! Don't you have any manners?" The woman didn't acknowledge the remark and continued with her chore as she sang along to a song playing loudly on her radio. Valentina smiled and began humming along. Her tram was about to leave and she made a dash for it. She jumped on and scouted for a seat, spotting one toward the back, and taking her seat, which required negotiating around a man whose head was buried in his newspaper. She took out a book from her purse and began reading. The woman sitting next to her got up, preparing to get off the bus.

"Signorina, may I sit next to you?" Paolo asked smiling.

Valentina looked up from her book. She looked around nervously.

"What are you doing here?" she asked.

"I needed to get crosstown," he said. "This is the tram that will get me there."

"Well, all right, if that's what you're doing," she said as she continued reading her book.

"Valentina, please don't ignore me. I knew you would be on this tram. I needed to see you. I thought you might be happy seeing me too," Paolo said.

"Two months, Paolo! Two months of expecting you to be outside the shop and now you want me to be happy? I'm not sure you heard, but I'm getting married in two days."

Clearly sounding frustrated he tried to explain. "I gave

my word to Antonio that I would stay away." Then gently he continued, "I wanted so much to see you again."

Valentina sighed wearily and closed her book.

"Two days…" Paolo reflected. "Then you made your decision? You are going through with it?"

Valentina didn't reply but looked at Paolo wanting to tell him how happy she was to see him, how she imagined this moment, seeing him again, but the words didn't come out.

But Paolo understood, nodding his head and smiling. "We still have time," he said.

As if they were completely alone, Paolo kissed her. Valentina didn't resist. She then looked around, but no one seemed to be paying attention to them. She smiled and touched her lips. And then looked at her hands.

"Paolo, it's all too late," Valentina said. She had to find a way to make all this go away and even if she was speaking these words to Paolo, she was really trying to convince herself. "After all, nothing really happened—we had lunch, we kissed a couple of times, kid's stuff."

"You are wrong. You know that. It's much more than that—if it wasn't I wouldn't be here and you wouldn't have thought about me all this time. And you were wrong about another thing, Valentina—that day in Portofino you told me we didn't have choices, but we do have choices. I have the choice to say no to working with my father, and I certainly have a choice of who I love and with whom I want to spend the rest of my life with, in spite of what my parents think or wish for me. And you have a choice of whom you marry. You must see that?"

"Paolo, I can even say that I love you, but that doesn't make it all perfect. For someone like me it's better sometimes to just wish for something instead of having it come true and then taken away. Where would I go from there?"

"The only reason it wouldn't work is if you fell out of love with me. I know I will always feel the same about you. We will never agree on everything, but we can have a lifetime together to figure it all out. I will wait for you until the last possible moment, you still have a choice and a decision to make."

"My stop is coming up," Valentina said.

"I know, I've been here with you many times," Paolo said. As he reached for her hand, they looked at each other's eyes, their differences no longer existed—the truth was there and Valentina couldn't deny it. But she pulled away as the tram stopped, quickly heading to the opening doors.

"I will wait for you, always!" Paolo yelled.

Valentina didn't look back as the tram drove away.

Two days later, Valentina stood dressed in her mother-in-law's wedding gown looking at herself in the mirror. Ilaria fussed with the veil.

Get that look out of your eyes, you made your choice, Valentina thought—but even at that moment she knew she was lying to herself. She hadn't stopped thinking of Paolo for a moment. She could still feel his hand squeezing hers.

"You look so beautiful," Ilaria said. "But why the sad

face?"

"I..." Valentina paused then said, "I wish my mother and father were here today."

"I understand. But I'm sure they are looking down at you from heaven. I know they are."

Valentina looked at her hand rubbing the callouses on her fingers, and then she slipped on white satin gloves, picked up the sides of the dress and marched toward the door, then stopped and turned, looking at her reflection in the mirror, her hair pulled back, her make-up light and unnoticeable. The dress had been altered to resemble that of Elizbeth Taylor's dress in the movie *Father of the Bride*: long sleeves, a sweetheart neckline and lots of lace had been added. "It is beautiful," Valentina whispered, "but I feel like an imposter." At that moment she really wished her parents were there to rescue her.

Family and guests were waiting in the hallway of the apartment and all along the staircase of the building. The bride would walk with her matron of honor beside her holding the bride's bouquet, and together they would lead the procession to the church located four blocks away. As Valentina appeared exiting the front door of Renaldo's family's apartment, applause broke out.

Valentina had been given a choice to ride the three blocks in a horse drawn carriage or go by car. She had dismissed the idea of the carriage when she heard what it would cost.

"For that much I will pull the carriage to the church!" Valentina had said.

Instead, she had chosen to walk. She'd told Renato that

she liked the idea of the procession. It reminded her of how things had been done in Locorotondo. Brides would emerge from their houses to a shower of paper confetti tossed by children. Then the children danced around them as they headed toward the church which stood prominently at the top of the town's main street.

Paolo had parked on the side of the road close to the church. The red flashy vehicle stood out and so did he, in an exquisite blue suit that cost as much as a month's wages for some of the guests walking into the church. In the two days since seeing Valentina on the bus Paolo had shared everything with his parents, explaining to them that he would try till the last possible moment to get her back.

"You hardly know this girl. How can you make a decision so important on a whim?" his mother had said.

His father had been more direct. "You are behaving like a child. Don't you have any self-respect?"

"I know you have always given me everything I ever wanted, but this is not a whim, I know what I feel for this girl. I wouldn't have any respect for myself if I didn't try," Paolo responded.

Even after threats of being disinherited, Paolo stood firm. "If I succeed in getting her back, she will become my wife. You can either gain a daughter or lose a son."

Paolo stood leaning on his car trying not to notice people staring at him as they walked by. He wrapped and unwrapped

Valentina's foulard, much like Valentina had done the first day they had met.

Paolo now knew what Renato looked like. He and Antonio, his best man, arrived at the church. Paolo noticed that Renato wasn't very tall, he had dark features and the build of a weightlifter, his walk reminded Paolo of a small gorilla, shifting side to side as he made his way, giving Paolo and his car a quick glance, not seeming to have an opinion on either the man or his vehicle. Antonio nonchalantly waved at Paolo. Paolo tentatively waved back. Antonio then leaned over and said something to Renato as he smiled and patted him on the back as they entered the church.

Valentina appeared as she turned the corner, making her way up the small incline of the street toward the church. Paolo could hear honking of cars and people yelling "Congratulations!"

And then Valentina saw Paolo. Even with the veil draped over her face Paolo could see her expression as she stopped to regard him. She didn't seem surprised. She took a deep breath looking somewhat relieved and then she smiled. Paolo watched Ilaria as she said something to Valentina. Valentina replied and grabbed the sides of her dress as if she was in some sort discomfort. Ilaria fussed with the dress, straightening the train, and Valentina resumed walking, at a much slower pace, then stopped. She leaned over to Ilaria, whispering something in her ear. Valentina then veered toward Paolo, leaving Ilaria looking confused. Valentina stopped a few feet from Paolo.

Valentina smiled as tears streamed down her face. "You

are so handsome, Mr. Deluca," she whispered.

Paolo opened the door on the passenger side of the car, inviting her in with a bow of his head.

"I'm sorry," she whispered. "Thank you for giving me something that will always be mine and that no one will ever be able to take away."

"Valentina," Paolo called out, "Please!"

She then quickly made her way to Ilaria and the doors of the church. She stopped once more, turned and glanced at Paolo a final time. Ilaria positioned the hem and train of the gown and Valentina entered the church.

Paolo slowly closed the door of the car and then walked around to the driver's side. He sat in the car, unsure of what he should do. As he turned the key, the engine immediately responded, and he noticed Valentina's foulard still wrapped around his hand. He sat there with the engine idling, staring at his hand.

He began to drive slowly down the road Valentina had just walked on, but then he picked up speed and began zig-zagging through traffic, ignoring signals and the threats from screaming officers directing traffic. He veered and rocketed to Via Aurelia and there increased his speed, jamming the car into fifth gear and standing on the accelerator until the speed-ometer read sixty-five miles per hour. The engine demanded more, and he shifted to sixth. At eighty, he unfurled the fou-lard, held it for a moment, wanting to release it, but instead he braked hard and yanked the car to the gravel shoulder. He stomped the parking brake on, killed the engine, and got out.

Genoa was behind him, and he looked back at the city as if for the first time. He had never noticed the cranes, the new buildings coming up, the city seemed to be growing, expanding, becoming new.

He was awoken from this vision by a young man walking in the ditch, wearing brown shabby trousers and a shabby blazer, who stopped and regarded the car. "That's some ride you got there," he said with a heavy dose of jealousy in voice. Paolo looked at the young man for a long moment but said nothing—the lump in his throat too sore to speak. Instead he reached in his pocket, took out the keys, and tossed them, jangling like coins, to the shocked laborer who caught them as an eager bridesmaid catches a soaring bouquet.

"It's yours," Paolo said.

The man stood there sputtering, turning his head left and right as if trying to wake from a dream.

Paolo turned and faced the city again, and slowly walked toward it.

Acknowledgements

To Benjamin Obler, the best teacher, editor and friend one could hope for. Without his support, patience, encouragement, and guidance I never would would been able to get this work done.

To my niece, Marianna Campese, whose support and encouragement were paramount in my decision to once again sit down and write, I thank you from the bottom of my heart. Your input has been invaluable.

To my husband, Jorge Soto Vega for making me understand that I was not leaving a career behind, but I was finally making my dream come true. Thank you.

To my sisters and friends who listened to my frustration, shared my excitement and always, always encouraged me to keep writing, thank you. To those who have helped me put this book together, you guys are amazing: Marina Campese, Enza Maniscalco, Mina Stella, Kathleen Butler, Alvin Walker, Cody Sisco, Damian Korman, Vincent Puleo, and to Elianna Campese Korman, the most promising writer I know.

www.ingramcontent.com/pod-product-compliance
Lightning Source LLC
Chambersburg PA
CBHW022147240626
47153CB00007B/2548